Wherever

Lily  Goes

Sherry Boas

Caritas Press

Wherever Lily Goes

Sherry Boas

Cover and book design: Sherry Boas

For information regarding permission, contact:
Sherry Boas

First Edition, 2011

10 9 8 7 6 5 4 3 2 1

ISBN: 978-0-9833866-1-2

Published by Caritas Press, Phoenix, Arizona

For reorders and other inspirational materials visit our website at LilyTrilogy.com

For Liz, my "editor" and my "Ethel," who talks me out of all my harebrained ideas, inspires the good ones and never turns down a cup of coffee.

Wherever Lily Goes is the second in a trilogy available from Caritas Press.

Until Lily
Wherever Lily Goes
Life Entwined with Lily's

"Now, more than ever, the world needs to hear the messages embedded in the Lily trilogy, which so beautifully, candidly and, at times, humorously, captures the incredible sacrifices and unmatched reward of parenthood. This is a story, not just for those with special needs children, but for all parents who struggle in one way or another. And isn't that pretty much all parents?"
– Father Doug Lorig, creator of *A Spirituality of Parenting* video series.

"I could not put these books down! Ms. Boas captures the raw emotion and secret thoughts of the human heart and pours them out into novels which will make people think, question, and no doubt view the sanctity of every life with more value. The depth of the characters and the very real situations they encounter draw the reader into story lines that touch on every point of human life – from conception to death – with humor, tenderness and, above all, a realness sure to penetrate anyone lucky enough to find these gems." – Kristina L. Forbes, mother of seven and former Director of Counselor Training, Aid to Women Center

"The Lily Trilogy is a heartwarming look at life through the lens of pure love. Lily touches your soul in an inspiring way that only one so close to God truly can." -- Tom Peterson, President and Founder, Virtue Media and Catholics Come Home

Visit www.lilytrilogy.com

Contents

1

PARALLELS

I spent the afternoon wracking my brain, trying to remember why I didn't marry Don Simon. I would have never had to change another light bulb as long as I live. Or brew another pot of coffee or even pour it in my cup. Or stir in my sugar. That man thought of everything. I came home from work one evening to find someone had installed a new rust-free mailbox and a "Live, Laugh and Love" welcome mat, replacing the old sisal, which had become shredded to the point of catching the toe of your shoe as you crossed the threshold. My porch light went on to reveal a note stuck into my door jam. It was written in large, flamboyant cursive.

"An automatic light to keep my friend safe, a door mat to remind her what life is all about after a long hard day, and a mailbox to receive the letters of loved ones."

He referred to me as "friend" because that's what I insisted upon. Once in the silky pink dawn following a satisfying stretch of all-night conversation, he kissed me on the lips and confirmed what I had always suspected. There would never be anything romantic between us.

Still, I think of Don Simon every time I have to replace the caulk in the shower or delay hanging a shelf because my drill isn't charged. Yes, I did say *my* drill. Jake is not the least bit interested in being handy. This afternoon, he squeezed past my ladder as I changed the batteries in the hallway smoke detector.

"Babe, hurry with that," he called from the stairwell. "The playoffs are on. You can't miss this."

For three years, I was pursued by a man who anticipated my every need in meticulous detail and fulfilled desires I didn't even know I had. Did I mention that the mailbox Don Simon surreptitiously installed was an original design, which he hand made to look like a birdhouse because he and I often went bird watching together? For nine mornings after the new mailbox, I awoke to find the flag raised and a small bone china bird inside it. I don't know why nine. I think that was probably all the species Lenox made.

But I chose as a life-long mate a man who never seems to notice that the room is a little on the dim side. I chose a man who considers it his contribution to home maintenance when he puts a new roll of toilet paper on the spindle. I chose a man who would never even think of trying to remember how many sugars I take in my coffee or whether I am willing to drink Coffee-mate in the absence of half and half. I chose Jake Lovely because I found Don Simon's thoughtfulness annoying at best and pathological at its scariest. I had the creepy feeling I was being stalked by his goodness. Underlying his attentions, I was sure, was an underhanded alter ego, sneaking around in the dark of night to do good, trying to win me over by deed because his words had been unsuccessful in persuading my passions that he was the man I should marry. That I told him there was no chemistry, didn't faze him. There was plenty on his side for the both of us, he said. Looking back on it, on days like today, I realize lack of chemistry is a ridiculous reason not to marry a man who has dedicated hours of his time to you at a workbench, whispering your name with each raspy passing of his saw.

Of course, I have no way of knowing if Don Simon would have flung his body over mine in a field of flying bullets, but that's not the criteria by which I married anyway. I married Jake for chemistry, which many married couples can affirm, fades faster than new car smell. Anyway, in the practical day-to-day of life, the only chemistry that is really imperative is the kind that removes mildew from grout lines.

But I didn't turn from romantic to pragmatic overnight. This is what happens to a woman after seventeen years of marriage to a man who doesn't notice she has donated twelve inches of her hair to Locks of Love.

Jake asks questions but never listens to the answer. His questions are polite and general. "How was your day? What are the kids up to? Any news from the home front?" But never once does he ask anything about what color schemes I am cooking up for my clients or how they liked the results. I don't think he understands the value of my work. To tell the truth, I don't either sometimes. But I pour all my creative energy into it, and it sometimes occurs to me that Don Simon would have wanted to know every last detail -- not in general terms like, did I use jewel tones or pastels? But specifics. Was it Caribbean Coral or Mexican Chili Pepper that I'd settled on for Mrs. Tremont's dining room? Did I pair it with Honey Bear or Gold Bluff? What emotion was I trying to evoke? How did I know Mrs. Tremont was a warm shade person? How did I know Mr. Tremont wouldn't hate the lace tablecloth? How did I accentuate the architectural details in the space and what fabric had I chosen for the ceiling-to-floor curtains? He would have asked these questions, not because he cares a rat's you-know-what about interior design, but because he would have seen my work as a part of me -- an extension of my intellect or maybe even my soul.

Most women would never write what I'm writing, for fear that their husbands will read it. I, however, am at liberty. I know Jake Lovely, and he will not be the least bit interested in anything I might find to write about. It is not, after all, going to stream across the bottom of his television screen on an ESPN ticker.

If it wasn't for the fact that my heart momentarily stopped the first time I looked into Jake's eyes, I would probably have opted for a life of quiet chastity, living with my yellow dog in a run-down guest house on a large parcel of unkempt grass, cooking dinner once a week for a wannabe lover who would change my light bulbs. But Jake was -- and still is -- the most aesthetically beautiful man I have ever seen. To say he is handsome does not do him justice. You'd have to be six feet under to lack chemistry with such a man. The last I checked, I still have a pulse. And yet, I have watched my relationship with Jake change from lover to friend to nothing much at all. C.S. Lewis says the difference between lovers and friends is that lovers are face to face, absorbed in each other. And friends are side-by-side absorbed in a common interest. For me and Jake, the birth of our first child ushered in the friend phase. Our gaze turned from each other to the wonder and beauty of this amazing third that had miraculously sprung from our passion. But now, Jake and I are gazing at two unrelated points in space. I am ashamed to admit that I have fantasies -- or should I call them plans? -- of leaving after the kids are grown. We're only talking another eight years until our youngest is out of the house.

Jake and I used to know each other well, before we knew each other for so long. Instead of growing in knowledge of each other, we have grown in unfamiliarity. We have become two parallel lines, extending infinitely into eternity, but never intersecting. Because of the law of parallel lines, I know nothing can ever change that, save some spontaneous and mighty force that would bend one of us toward the other.

I don't know. Maybe I'm not technically marriage material. It took me quite a while to realize I even wanted to get married. From what I had witnessed growing up, it seemed to me men were either a heck of a lot of trouble, lying cheats or missing in action. And in some instances, all of the above. Uncle Jack comes to mind here. It was on more than one occasion that he would thwart Auntie Bev's efforts to establish some kind of order in our home. Then he blamed her for being too uptight and got hooked up with some bimbo at work. We kids saw him very little after that. I feel guilty that I didn't even cry at his funeral. But Lily did enough crying for all of us.

She's doing enough for Auntie Bev too. Lily's by herself in Seattle now since Auntie Bev died three months ago. Lily considered it her duty and her joy to visit Auntie Bev every day in the nursing home. Every day for seven years. Auntie Bev was Lily's life, and now Lily is going to have to find something else to live for.

These were the thoughts that occupied my Saturday afternoon -- the gradual dimming of a marriage and the sudden, engulfing darkness of grief. Then evening came and these two unrelated and unpleasant realities wove themselves together over beer and steak. I mentioned to Jake over dinner celebrating our seventeenth wedding anniversary that Mrs. Pendleton -- the owner of the group home -- hears Lily crying herself to sleep every night.

"Why don't we bring her out here," Jake said with a mass of baked potato and porterhouse stuffed into his left cheek. "You can do the attic into a bedroom." He spoke as if he was making a suggestion to invite a neighbor to a barbecue, but I knew something Jake didn't know. He could never grasp the enormity of what he was suggesting. How could he? He had no experience living with Lily. The longest stretch of time he'd spent with her was at weddings and funerals.

"Her case worker says she needs to stay where she's at, continue working, keep everything as normal as possible," I told Jake. "Too many changes at once could send her into a real depression."

"But she's got no family where she's at," Jake said, reaching past his glass of Guinness and forcing his fork into the slab of New York Strip I'd left unattended with an unspoken invitation for him to finish it. "That's got to be depressing."

The meat plopped off his fork on the way to his plate. He picked it up, tossed it on his plate, licked his fingers and pinched a white twill napkin between his forefinger and thumb. That man can eat anything he wants, and in large quantity. He's got one of those rare metabolisms that could convert a deep-fried Twinkie into solid muscle.

"Mmmm. That's good steak. You chose well."

"She's lived in Seattle all her life, though," I said. "I just don't see how it works to move her."

Jake just chewed. I watched his temple popping in and out.

"OK," he said, picking up his stein. "So we move there."

"What?"

He took two gulps of his beer. "Well, we've been wanting Beth to get away from these losers she's been hanging with."

I really couldn't think of a good argument. I could work anywhere. Jake could work anywhere. And the way things were going with Beth she might end up dead without some drastic change of course.

"Besides," Jake said, "aren't you tired of shoveling snow?"

I just looked at him stunned.

"You've always said you miss the ocean," he added.

"You're serious about this."

"Yeah. Let's make a new start. We'll do it for Lily. And for Beth. And I bet it won't be a bad deal for you and me either." He leaned in over his plate as if he were about to reveal a secret. "Something new. Get us out of our rut."

"Our rut."

"Yeah," he winked and raised the glass to his lips, holding it there while his eyes smoldered with the heat of a distant desire. "It's time for a change."

****

The nice thing about being an interior designer is you really don't have to change much to make your house show well. We got our asking price in nine days. That was the day we called Lily to tell her we were moving out to live with her.

All my friends had the same reaction. I never considered my husband a dragon slayer, but everyone was amazed that he would uproot his life and sign up to take care of a woman with Down Syndrome.

PARALLELS

"You've got a real gem in Jake," said my best friend, Frannie Jones, who was well aware that Jake Lovely has never changed a light bulb since the day we were married. "I would never be able to convince my husband to do anything like what Jake is doing for you."

Suddenly, as if I had traded the old one in for a new model, I am married to a gallant man. Who, by the way, informed me on the day we left for Seattle that I had missed patching some nail holes in the hallway.

Laura and Katie are excited for a new adventure, especially one that involves the Pacific shoreline. Beth practically went into convulsions, weeping and gnashing her teeth over leaving her friends, particularly one of the opposite sex named Travis. We told her now was the time to put our own needs aside and think of Lily. Now was the time to do something heroic. She still cried, but she had few arguments that could carry any weight beside a helpless, sad, frightened, vulnerable soul who needs her family.

Our first evening on the road, we found Beth in the motel lobby plotting her escape, looking up on-line bus schedules back to Minneapolis and a map of how to get to the nearest Greyhound terminal. After that, I set up the rollaway at the door and slept all night as a human barricade. At the next motel, we were invaded at dusk when one of the kids, trying to retrieve a pair of sunglasses, moved a night stand, apparently disturbing a nest of crickets. It was like one of those ridiculous science fiction movies where maybe the crickets get into some kind of radioactive waste that gives them a mind for violence. They were big and brown -- the largest crickets I had ever seen -- and it occurred to me I was probably dreaming. They came at us from what seemed like every direction, springing themselves over and over onto the musty green carpet, as if they were trying to gain height on a trampoline. Beth climbed up in the middle of the bed, grabbed herself around the knees, rocked back and forth and wept as if someone had died. I put my arms around her and told her it was healthy to have a good cry and that I understood that

7

she was suffering many losses. I resisted the temptation to add the next part of what I was thinking -- that she was about to score a few gains too. New friends, the beach, a fresh start devoid of all judgments that people pass about party girls and stoners -- that they are depressing and a little scary. Subhuman. Like ghosts rattling around inside old boarded-up houses.

I suppose if I hadn't known Beth all her life, I would have thought the same. If all I had known of her is a snapshot of 15-year-old angst -- pierced navel and tattooed backside -- I could have passed the same judgments. But mothers don't deal in snapshots. Mothers are all about streaming video. Mothers see the cumulative, not the transient. They see what their child is, was and might become all in a single flash. Every bit as much as my child is the pale, raccoon-eyed, raven-haired heap of hormonal misery who reeks of cigarettes and tells me she hates me, she is also the small girl with sunshine glinting off her yellow hair, chasing bubbles, snatching them from the air with her chubby wide-spread fingers, giggling at the audacity bubbles have of popping in your face. It's not that I haven't noticed that somewhere along the line, something has rubbed the shine clean off my Beth -- something tenacious and abrasive. It's just that, mothers know that all things can be restored to their original luster, given the right agent.

We arrived in Seattle at sunset on the third day, and somehow, someway, by some not-so-small miracle, Beth arrived with us.

We showed up at Lily's group home just as the house was sitting down for dinner. I've never been hugged like that in my life. I'm quite certain the last time I was in such physical pain it was because Jake had gotten me to Labor and Delivery too late for an epidural. Lily squeezed me so hard, my feet levitated. I was so happy to see her, I didn't want to tell her I couldn't breathe, and I couldn't have anyway, given the lack of air to push through my vocal cords. As the sister of someone with Down Syndrome, I was accustomed to the momentary losses of lung capacity, otherwise known as love. I just forgot how much it hurt. And how good it felt to be loved so deeply.

"Tewry!" she squealed.

She set me down and led me by the arm into the dining room. "Everyone, everyone. This my sister, Tewry. She my big sister from when I was a kid and she was a kid. And we had a brother Jimmy, too. Where's Jimmy, Tewry? Where's Jimmy?"

"He's still in Denver, Lily," I told her. I re-introduced her to Jake and the kids, and she gave each one a hug and a kiss. "I love you guys," she said. "I got a picture of you."

"We have a picture of you too," Jake said. "It's very pretty. But it's not as pretty as you are in person."

"Than- you," Lily blushed. "I got a picture of Daddy, too. I gonna visit him when I get money. He live in California. Maybe you come too."

"Sure, I'll go to California," Laura said.

"Universal Studios!" said Katie. "Oh, can we, Dad? Please?"

"Maybe if you girls eat all your spinach every day for a year," he said.

"Oh, Daddy," Katie said. "I hate spinach."

"Does quiche count?" Laura asked.

"Not in my universe," Jake said.

"Why not?" Laura said.

"My universe. My standards," he smiled. "Does easy listening count as music in yours?"

"OK. No quiche."

As I watched Lily clamp her arms around Jake's solid mid-section, it became clear to me that I had almost certainly been robbed of all future options. Jake's willingness to uproot his life solved an immediate problem and created a long-term one. Yes, my sister will be taken care of and my daughter might be plucked from the jaws of destruction. But this solution comes at a price. And a mighty hefty one at that. I will have to sacrifice an entire future of emotional fulfillment for this plan, because as anyone with half a heart will tell you, a wife does not leave a

husband after he has committed such a selfless act of perfect generosity. Unless she can build a very serious case against him on
a whole other level, she will have no hope of exiting the marriage. I can't imagine what circumstance might justify my
departure from this day forward, although one may exist. If it
does, it will not go unnoticed.

2

THE WEAK LINK

We are looking for a house with an easy bus route to the Woodland Park Zoo because of Lily's budding painting career. She specializes in animals of prey. I remember she and Jimmy used to watch DVDs of *Wild Animal Kingdom* for hours. I can still see them, sitting there on the couch together. Jimmy's arm around Lily, twisting the ends of her hair through his fingers. I don't remember exactly when it was that Lily agreed to such an arrangement. For many years, messing with her hair was strictly prohibited by Lily, who learned the "all done" sign specifically so she could use it on Jimmy, who had always found the silkiness of her hair irresistible. Sign language never really worked on Jimmy. But there finally came a day when Mom was suddenly and momentarily grateful for Jimmy's unrelenting fascination with Lily's hair because it was the unwitting inspiration for her first word: "shthTop!"

Virtually every home we've seen since we've started house hunting has had some combination of canary yellow and brick red interior walls. What is wrong with these people? Have they never watched an episode of the Unsellables on HGTV? Color is nice, but these homes look like they've been decorated by Dr. Seuss. *Wocket in my Pocket* comes to mind. We are putting an offer on a large home that the owners claim has been newly updated. But there is only one time period that I know of when dusty rose carpeting, mauve countertops and white-washed cabinets would have been acceptable and that was the 1980s. Fortunately, I can see through to the bones of a house. With its garish color scheme, it's been sitting on the market for quite a while, so hopefully the owners will snap up our offer. Then I can work my magic. I'm partial to the Tuscan interiors that were popular at the turn of the century. I don't care what anyone says. There is such a thing as objective beauty and Tuscany embodies it. You can say it's not your style, you can say you don't want to live with it, you can say you've grown tired of it, but you cannot say, with any intellectual sincerity, that it is not beautiful.

The 1980s house has a nice neighborhood. Tire swings dangling over crew-cut lawns, Adirondack chairs on clean-swept porches, a bow rider boat in an occasional driveway. No broken-down pickups parked in beds of weeds. There is, however, one thing about the neighborhood that gives us pause. A middle-aged woman three houses down watched us drive by while the water streamed from her hose onto her azaleas. In the drizzling rain.

Auntie Bev once told us that in every neighborhood she'd ever lived there was at least one of these such ladies, equipped with an arsenal of highly- effective techniques designed to gather information about each neighbor and distribute it freely to people whose business it is not. This self-appointed, unofficial neighborhood herald will, for example, prune her shrubs with small and meticulous snips, all the while watching from under her wide-brimmed hat the rising and setting of neighborhood affairs, hoping to spot something atypical and noteworthy. She takes long strolls, sometimes twice a day, which is how she has managed to meet every living being in a two-mile radius. She has an impeccable memory for names, including those of children and pets. She always has time to stop and chat.

She is accomplished at giving the impression that you are the only one who is receiving her treasured tidbits of gossip. She comes close to you in a hushed voice and sometimes even lays a hand on your forearm. But you are well aware that she is dropping your neighbor's business with you, picking up yours and dropping it at the next house. I grew up understanding that you never tell your secrets to anyone who has told you someone else's. Auntie Bev put it this way: "A dog who will bring a bone will take one too." But it doesn't matter that you know this. If you engage in any kind of conversation whatsoever with your neighborhood herald, you're going to unwittingly give her something she can use.

Our house back in Minneapolis had a garage and a blocked in backyard. With that kind of arrangement, if you drive in and close your garage door before leaving your vehicle, you never have to catch a glimpse of another human soul, nor let anyone catch a glimpse of you. This is what Jake and I did for the first two years. It wasn't until Beth came along that we met our first neighbor. When you have children, you begin to use your front door. The stroller passes through it, like thread through the eye of a needle, sewing you into the fabric of a neighborhood that, up until then, had left you unfettered on its fringe. That's when you learn that you've been living three houses down from the neighborhood herald, who has been exceedingly frustrated with her own failure to glean any information from your address. Upon seeing you finally emerge, she quickly sets out to make up for lost time.

"This neighborhood has dubbed you the 'mystery couple on the corner,'" she told me one day while out for a walk with Beth. "We didn't even know you'd had a baby. We could have thrown you a shower!"

So as not to sound like the unneighborly, anti-social people that we were, I told her we both have very demanding jobs and were a little surprised how much work was involved in keeping up with a house as big as ours.

She popped her head under the stroller's visor and picked up Beth's hand. The baby's rubbery fingers curled around the woman's index finger as if they were old friends. "Isn't she precious! She has your eyes. Is she a good baby? Does she sleep through the night?"

"Not yet," I said. "Soon, I hope."

"Oh, you must be exhausted."

"Never been more tired in my life," I said.

From then on, we became known as the work-aholics who are living beyond our means and struggling to adjust to the rigorous demands of parenthood.

With this new house, I'm making a new start. There's nothing we can do if the neighborhood wants to tally the number of times Lily has to be returned to the house in a squad car after a 1 a.m. walk in search of the cemetery for a visit to Auntie Bev's grave. But I'd rather not have it keeping track of what drug treatment program our teenager is entering next. I'd really rather be labeled "mysterious." Yes, just in case Auntie Bev has passed on the curse of the neighborhood herald, we will be exiting and entering solely through the garage in this new house.

****

We decided to transfer Lily's account to a branch near us so she could do her banking when we did ours. The round-faced teller who helped us was in her early 20's, squeezed into a royal blue rayon suit with a bright yellow daisy lapel pin. She smiled at Lily and then proceeded to address all her questions to me.

"How do you spell the name? What's the address? Do you want a phone number on the checks?"

On the way home, Lily was quiet.

"You picked some very pretty checks," I told her. She gave me a slight smile.

"What's wrong, Lily?" I asked.

"How come that lady only talk to you, but it my money?"

"A very good question," I said. "She's young and she's probably never met anyone with Down Syndrome before. She doesn't know how smart you are."

"Do I look dumb?"

"Of course not, Lily."

Every once in a while, Lily becomes aware of aesthetics. In those moments she realizes she doesn't quite look like everyone else. I don't know if she would be able to tell you exactly why -- that her chin is thicker, her ears positioned lower, her eyes set behind lids stretched tight at the corners. That her feet trod far apart in her gait, that her two first toes have enough room between them for at least one other. I don't know if she could articulate all those specifics, but she knows she is different. Even as a little girl, she knew when she saw another person with Down Syndrome that she had found someone like herself. One time, when she was about 8, we went swimming at the public pool on opening day when admission was free. The place was mobbed. But Lily was able to find the one other child there who had Down Syndrome. She singled him out for a game of water tag and played with him the whole time.

When we got home from the bank, Katie wanted to know if Lily had picked up any lollipops. She actually had gotten two and eaten them on the way home.

"I sawry," she said to Katie.

"That's OK, Aunt Lily," Katie said. "Did you put your money in the bank?"

"Yeah. I got cool checks. Wanna see?"

"Sure."

Lily was proud that Katie expressed her approval of the checks, each of which had one of seven wild African animals. I remember the first checks Jake and I picked out together. He wanted Major League Baseball and I wanted Feathered Friends. We settled on a monogram "L." We spent our first year making compromises like that. Thereafter, Jake let me do pretty much whatever I wanted as long as it didn't interfere with his cable sports lineup.

"Did you get a credit card?" Katie asked Lily.

"Not yet."

"They're going to mail it," I said.

"When can I get one?" Katie asked me.

"When you get a job," I said.

"Can I go to the movies with Laura?" she asked, irrelevantly. "She said I could if you say it's OK."

"What's the movie?"

"*Wrecked.*"

"Honey, that's PG-13," I said. "You're 10."

"Please," she begged. "Trina saw it and said it was really good."

Auntie Bev and Uncle Jack used to take us to R-rated movies, not because of some philosophical ideal that children should not be kept in bubbles. Just because they couldn't find a babysitter. I remember Auntie Bev would bow her head and close her eyes if a scene got too violent. But she never covered our eyes. I always felt like we were doing something wrong by being there. I knew Mom would never have taken us. There were a lot of places Mom would have never taken us. She never took us to the drug store, for instance, because that's where sick people go to get their medicine. If a prescription needed to be filled, we went through the drive-through. Anything else that might have been on the shelves at the pharmacy was also available at less disease-laden places, so she thought, like the supermarket. Mom carried a bottle of hand sanitizer in her purse at all times, except when we went somewhere like a carnival or a petting zoo. At those types of places, she carried it in her hand. After each animal or after each ride, she'd give the command, "hands," and we'd obediently present our palms to her for a squirt of Purell, which Mom wouldn't have traded for equal parts of liquid gold. So, you can imagine how shocked we were when, one day, we saw our mother put her hands inside a public toilet. Lily had dropped her glasses in before she had managed to use the toilet, so the water was "clean." As clean as toilet water at a truck stop can be anyway.

Mom went to work as if she had previously thought out in minute detail exactly what she would do in such a situation and had run herself through mock drills. First, she grabbed a paper towel to turn on the faucet. This was always her habit. She didn't touch anything in a public restroom with her bare hands and there was a great penalty to pay if we ever dared to. It was a habit so ingrained that even though she was about to stick her hand inside a toilet, she could still not bring herself to touch the faucet. She turned the left handle as far as it would go, letting the water run, hoping for a stream of adequately hot water.

Then, she positioned herself over the toilet, one foot extended outside the stall, her hip propping the door open, ensuring there was nothing in the path between her and the sink. She rolled up her sleeve, furrowed her brow, pushed her upper lip up toward her nose and snatched the glasses from the water, quickly as if the water were hot and might burn her. She brought the contaminated spectacles out between her first finger and thumb, dripping and extended in front of her as far as they would go.

"Stand back!" she yelled at us. We moved swiftly and in perfect unison, the three of us, as if she were holding a scorpion by the tail. Not because we were afraid of the germs as much as we were afraid of the woman holding them. When it came to anything related to microorganisms, you didn't mess around with our mother. Her word was obeyed and obeyed quickly at such moments, and probably, as I look back on it, only at such moments.

Jimmy and I just looked at each other, and Lily watched with her mouth hanging open as Mom held the glasses under hot water and lectured Lily about never doing what she herself had just done.

"Never, never put your hand in a potty, OK Lily? Mommy just did that to get your --." She stopped mid sentence and held up the glasses, slightly above her head, looking through them. "Oh for crying out loud, Lily. The lens is missing. This is the fourth pair of glasses this year. You've got to be more careful."

Jimmy ducked into the stall and hollered, "Mom, Mom, here it is. Here's her lens."

I ran into the stall. There it was, sunk to the bottom of the toilet, in the hole where unspeakably disgusting things -- perhaps hundreds a day -- pass. Mom wouldn't dare. Would she?

She would. And she did. With the determined look of Aragorn sleighing orcs, she fished that lens out of there, popped it back in the frames, washed the glasses four or five times with hot soapy water, applied hand sanitizer to their entirety and washed them again. Then she went after her hands. I could have sworn I saw steam rising from the water that was streaming over her hands. The skin on them, usually a creamy white, turned a bright, unnatural pink.

"I will never be able to eat finger food again," she said.

It was at that moment that I realized how much our mother loved her children.

After that incident, Lily began a daily ritual of bathing her doll baby in the toilet. Fortunately, she used anti-bacterial soap.

Germ phobia is a familial trait, at least among same-gender siblings. Auntie Bev also suffered from it, although it was a bit milder than Mom's. It didn't help poor Auntie Bev, though, that, for an entire decade, the Center for Disease Control was constantly issuing warnings on the next pandemic. The winter that I turned 10, health officials were wringing their hands over the fourth mutation of the swine flu as waves of flu sufferers flooded emergency rooms with respiratory difficulties. Auntie Bev pointed the remote at the TV, flicked off the news and announced, "Well, kids, the last place I'm taking any of you is to the doctor or the hospital, so you better stay well and safe."

"How come?" asked Jimmy.

"All the sick people are there," she said. "If we go there, we'll get sick. So, no well checks this year with Dr. Hansen. I'm not taking a perfectly healthy child to the doctor to pick up a bunch of germs."

This was bad news for us. Once we had passed vaccination age, we loved going to the doctor. It was always fun hearing her make a big deal over how much we've grown, and she had a treasure box from which we could pick a really cool cheaply-made, nondurable plastic toy that Auntie Bev would immediately snatch from us and slather with germ killer before letting us have it back.

Auntie Bev had a theory that pediatricians are somehow akin to dishonest mechanics, who ensure repeat business by rigging one thing to break while they have your car in the shop fixing another. Why else, she reasoned, would doctors put toys and books in their waiting rooms for all the sick kids to handle and pass on to the next patient? And the playground outside of the office. How could they account for that? Doctors know how illnesses are spread. Some kid coughs into his hand and makes his way across the monkey bars. The next kids come along and there you go -- the latest plague is underway. We would always beg to play at Dr. Hansen's, vowing not to touch our faces until we were finished playing and had properly sanitized our hands. Auntie Bev was too savvy to enter into that kind of agreement.

"There's no such thing as a kid who doesn't have at least one bad germ-spreading habit," she'd say. "You're either a thumb sucker, nail biter, eye rubber or nose picker. Or, in some cases, Mr. Jimmy Greeley, all of the above. And no well-intentioned promises are going to keep you from infecting yourself."

But on the day in question, when the news had reported several more Swine Flu deaths in the Seattle area, Jimmy was going to press the issue. He was going to make Auntie Bev realize how ridiculous was her plan to stay away from all medical personnel and facilities until flu season had passed.

"What if we get hurt?" Jimmy asked. "Like what if we get stampeded by a herd of wildebeest or something?"

"If nothing is falling off, we'll put a band-aid on it and go on our merry way," she said.

Of course, with that kind of set up, you can guess where we spent our day. Lily had this habit of putting her fingers inside the door jamb as she stood in the doorway, waiting for someone to come out of a room. Auntie Bev was always hollering at her to get her fingers out. She had many times predicted that one day Lily would lose a finger. Her prediction came true on the day that Auntie Bev had forbidden us to suffer any medical emergencies. Jimmy was in hysterics as he watched Auntie Bev holding Lily's finger together. It was he who had closed the door on poor Lily's pinky. I had to take over the task of holding on to her finger, now wrapped in a towel, while Auntie Bev drove. Lily was trying to take off the towel and we were all afraid the fingertip, which was hanging by a thread, would be pulled all the way off with it. Jimmy blubbered uncontrollably the whole way. As we pulled into the ER parking lot, I searched the rear view mirror for Auntie Bev's reaction to the scene that lay before us. The ER was so full, patients were spilled into the parking lot, all wearing blue surgical masks. It may not have been Armageddon, but for a germ freak like Auntie Bev, it was as close to the end of the world as you could get.

There was no way Auntie Bev was going to let any part of our bodies or apparel touch any part of that waiting room. She chose us a place to stand and wait, near a small foyer in front of the double doors leading to the examining area, strategically as far away as possible from the people wrapped in blankets and coughing up pieces of lung. She held Lily in her arms, Lily's towel-wrapped finger gently pressed between them, her sad red face buried in Auntie Bev's neck.

We watched as one woman used a tissue to pick up the courtesy phone and another one to wrap around her index finger and dial.

Auntie Bev whispered in my ear. "Finally, everyone is coming around to my way of thinking. I actually feel quite comfortable here."

Right after that, another caller walked right up to the phone, picked it up with her bare hand, held it to her ear, dialed and rummaged through her purse while waiting for an answer. She pulled out a roll of life savers, peeled the paper to expose three of them and *touched* them all, before deciding on the green one at the bottom.

We all shifted from one foot to the other uneasily.

Auntie Bev and I shot each other a look when a woman pulled her mask off, coughed into her hand, and then put her mask back on. We read each other's minds.

"What's wrong with these people?" she thought.

"People are idiots," I thought back.

Although I was certain I hadn't touched anything, I began to feel germs crawling all over me.

Finally, it was Lily's turn to get checked in. The woman at the computer, behind the desk, clamped an oxygen monitor on Lily's finger and said, "Let's get her into the system."

We never did figure out why Lily had to wear an oxygen monitor for a severed finger, but the fact that she did touched off a significant and unfortunate series of events.

"Do you sterilize this monitor?" Auntie Bev asked.

"Oh, I sterilize *everything*," the woman said. "Look around. This is Germ Central."

"Yes. So, right before you put this on my daughter's finger, you wiped it down?"

"Well, I don't have time to do it every time," she said. "I mean, look around. This place is mobbed. I don't have time to wipe it down *every* time."

"Thank you for telling me," Auntie Bev replied, grabbing the germ killer from the outside pocket of her purse. I know if there had been such a thing as a holster for germ killer, Auntie Bev would have worn one. She was as fast on the draw as The Waco Kid.

"Last name of patient?"

"Greeley," Auntie Bev said, slathering germ killer onto Lily's hand. "Why are we wearing these ridiculous masks?"

"Have you not heard of the Swine Flu pandemic?"

"Have you not heard how the swine flu is transmitted? Hand to mouth, Sweetheart. What good do masks do if you're going to put the same germy apparatus on every infected patient's finger and then clamp it onto my daughter's, who if you haven't noticed has Down syndrome, and thus a compromised immune system?"

"Ma'am, the virus is also airborne." She was getting increasingly annoyed. "That's why we wear the masks. I'm doing the best I can here, but as you can see, we are extremely busy." She poised her red fingernails over the keyboard. "First name of patient?"

"Lilian. Infecting everyone who comes through the door is the best you can do? Look, Honey, if you think you're busy today, you ain't seen nothing." It was the first and only time I ever heard Auntie Bev use bad grammar. "Just wait until these germs you've been spreading incubate and see what kind of day you have Friday."

"Address?"

Auntie Bev wasn't about to let this one go. "Look, the wipes are right here." She pointed at a container on the counter within arm's reach that said, "Germ-Rid Antibacterial Wipes." Touching it was out of the question, as microorganisms would surely be lying in wait on a surface such as that.

"Look, if you're not happy here, you can go to urgent care," the woman behind the computer said. "But we really need to move this along. Some of these people have been waiting six hours to see a doctor. You're lucky someone's bleeding or you'd still be sitting there too. Now, could I have the address please?"

Auntie Bev gave the woman the rest of the requested information and collected a little of her own too. This issue was not going to die any quicker than those highly contagious, extremely virulent flu germs. I would later find out that Auntie Bev had every intention of making that woman's name known all the way up to the hospital's board of directors.

Five days after our trip to the ER, Jimmy was sick with fever and body aches. He was the weak link in our family. He was the one who was untrainable in the war on germs. Mom had been successful in teaching the rest of us how to use the restroom without touching anything. Even Lily wadded up a piece of toilet paper and pressed the flusher with it. But as many times as Mom explained to Jimmy that people wipe their butts and then touch the flusher with their dirty hands, he still chose to put his fingers on it. It probably had more to do with his learning style than any stubbornness on his part. Aside from video games, whatever Jimmy learned one day, he had to re-learn the next.

THE WEAK LINK

Every spring at cherry season, Jimmy had to learn all over again that cherries have pits. Every fall, he had to learn why the harvest moon is orange. He had to learn each Lent that Easter is always on a Sunday, but not on the same date. And, believe it or not, as strange as this is for a kid, he had to learn each winter that Christmas is always on December 25. He had to learn that a year has 12 months, not 10, and a minute has 60 seconds and not 59, even though the count-down timer flips to 59 as soon as you press "go." He had to learn at least three times a week during math homework that a 1 and a 2 together is twelve, not twenty-one. At least that often, he had to learn that microwaves cook in minutes, not in hours. So it is not, in the final analysis, surprising that he is the one who got sick after that trip to the ER. He must have, at some point during the nine-hour incident, touched a door knob and rubbed his eyes when Auntie Bev's back was turned or grabbed a drink from the water fountain on his way back from the restroom. Or maybe it was the flusher.

3

WHEREVER LILY GOES

We got Lily in the car at 8:30 this morning.

"Where we goin?" she asked, as she wrestled her seatbelt over her round belly.

"It's a surprise," I told her.

"For my bir-day?"

"Yup."

"The movie?"

"No."

"To McDonald's?"

"Nope."

"Dancing?"

"At 9 o'clock in the morning, Lily?"

She grinned mischievously. "I love to dance."

"I know you do. But we're not going dancing."

"Where we goin'?"

"It's a surprise. I can't tell you."

"Please."

"You'll just have to wait," I said. "But you're going to like it. A lot."

"Please," she begged. "Tell me."

"OK," I said. "I'll tell you where we're going."

"You will?"

"We're going to the airport."

"We goin' on a trip?"

"I'm not saying any more, Lily," I said. "You'll just have to wait and see what the surprise is."

As we waited at the gate, Lily couldn't sit down. She paced in front of the windows watching the planes take off. Jake watched three different professional sporting events on his handheld.

"Life doesn't get any more suspenseful than this," I told Jake.

"I know," he said. "If the Vikings win this one, they go on to the Super Bowl."

"Oh, I'm sorry you have to be watching such an important game at the airport, Honey," I said.

"It's OK," he said. "We'll be home by the third quarter."

I sat there and wondered how a distant field of eleven strangers, whose lives revolve around a "ball" that doesn't even bounce correctly, could be more fascinating than what was about to transpire within a three-foot radius. But so it was to Jake Lovely, who seemed to make a hobby of living his life detached from anything and everything that had importance to the woman he promised to cherish for a lifetime. Is this the abandonment I was destined to endure until the day I die? Who could expect someone to see that through to the end? And yet, what would the divorce decree say? *True, Mr. Lovely cared enough about his wife to lay down his life for her disabled sister, but he watches too much football. The state of Washington does hereby declare the marriage between these two pitiable fools irretrievably broken.*

"Is that our plane?" Lily asked, pointing to a 747 taxiing down the runway.

"No, we're not going anywhere," I said.

She looked out the window again and just watched, confused. She pointed to a plane taking off.

"Is that our airplane?"

"No, Lily," I said, "But your surprise is almost here. It's coming on an airplane."

"Is it big?"

"Yes," I said.

"Like an elephant?"

"No," I said. "Not that big."

"Like a dog?"

"Better than a dog."

"A baby?"

"No, not a baby. They don't usually come on airplanes."

"I saw on TV one did."

"A baby came on an airplane?"

"Yeah. From a place. To a Mommy and a Daddy."

"Look," I said pointing out the window at a jumbo jet touching down. "There's the plane."

"It has my surprise?"

"Yup."

"Dang it!" Jake forced his words out through clinched teeth. "He fumbled."

Lily pressed her nose and forehead against the window. She kept it there, staring at the jet, until I laid my hand on her shoulder and said "Lily, look."

Ambling out of the jet way door was a leathery-faced, slightly rickety man whose wide smile radiated enough warmth to warrant its own weather report.

"Daddy!" Lily ran. Pablo Perez dropped his carry-on and opened his arms wide, planting his feet and steadying himself for the force of affection that was about to plow into him.

"Mija!" he exclaimed as he squeezed her tight. "I missed you Mijita."

When his eyes opened, I could see they were shiny with puddling tears.

"I miss you too," Lily said, still holding him firm around his middle, head on his chest. I worried that she was squeezing him too hard, but he didn't seem in pain. As a matter of fact, I'm not sure I've ever seen that much peace on anyone before.

"Happy birthday, Mijita," he said, cradling her face in his large hands and looking into her eyes. "Let me look at you. You look beautiful."

"Can you stay for dinner, Daddy?" Lily asked. "We having cake."

"You bet," he said winking at me. "How are you, Terry? You look wonderful." He reached one arm out to hug me, still not letting go of Lily. I wanted the kind of hug she had gotten, but I was going to have to settle for this. For now. Jake put his handheld down and shook his hand. The men exchanged brief greetings and a few words about the Vikings' chances of winning.

"So, Lily," Pablo said, returning both arms to her. "How many candles on your cake?"

"Um," she said. "Um." She looked at me.

"Thirty-seven." I said.

"Yeah," Lily said. "Thirty-seven."

"Oh, I remember thirty-seven," Pablo Perez said. "It was a very good year. You are lucky, my Lily, to be thirty-seven."

"I lucky cuz my Daddy here when I am 37," Lily said.

Pablo squeezed her tight. "Hey, you know what, Lily? I brought you something. But we're going to have to go to baggage claim to get it."

"OK," said Lily grinning.

"And Lily, you can thank your sister for allowing me to give you this gift," he said, smiling at me.

What was I going to say? How could I deny Lily the joy that comes from raising something little into something grown.

Pablo Perez had recently gotten into the business of dog breeding. He had finally, at the age of 64, been able to partially fulfill his life-long dream. When he was nine, growing up in Guaymas, he took in his first stray dog, wrapped its mangled paws with pieces of gauze he begged from Senor Sanchez de Leon at the drug store and fed it fallen grain he had scooped up from the dirt between the railroad ties. Hungry children in Guaymas lost their arms on that track, failing to get out of the way of the grain train, which unwittingly dropped small amounts of its contents -- irresistible sustenance to orphans who had been displaced onto the streets because their mothers had no more food and no more room in their cardboard shanties. Young Pablo kept his limbs, maybe because he was swift about his grain collection or maybe he was not so hungry. He was one of the fortunate ones with a roof over his head -- cardboard though it was. His stray dog, which he named "Caballero," meaning "Knight," recovered and inspired in him the desire to become a vet. That was an ambition that would never come to be, given the poverty that precluded him from an education. School was free, but uniforms and shoes were not, and his family could not afford them.

Now, at the far end of his life, he was at the Sea/Tac Airport, presenting his daughter with a home-bred bull terrier puppy in what might possibly have been one of the happiest moments of his life. It was a moment when luggage-laden travelers passed by three teary-eyed adults encircling a round-faced woman, sitting in the middle of the floor, answering back to the helpless yelps escaping from the purple crate in her lap.

"He want out," Lily said, peeking into the grate. She looked up at her father. "Can I take him out?"

"I don't know if that's a good idea, Lily," I said. "Let's wait until we get him home."

Pablo pulled a key out of his pocket and unlocked the kennel. "It's OK, Mija," he said to me. "This little rascal will do no harm in Lily's arms."

He gently brought the squirming puppy with one hand, which looked suitable for ditch digging or brain surgery. It was strong, steady and gentle, with prominent veins and obvious bones.

"He look like the Target dog," Lily said, engulfing the animal into her embrace. The puppy wriggled its way out over her arms and licked her on the mouth. She laughed hysterically.

"That's exactly what he is," Pablo said. "A bull terrier."

"I love him," Lily said, tilting her chin away from the dog's tongue. "He so cute. What his name?"

"That's for you to decide, Mija," Pablo said.

"I call him Pablo," Lily said.

"I'm honored," Pablo said, winking at me.

Pablo picked up his carry-on with one hand and put the other around Lily, who fit perfectly under his arm. It was halftime, so Jake snapped a shot of them while the puppy stretched his neck to get within licking distance of Lily's chin. Life was picking up where it left off 36 years ago. But this time, Pablo Perez was in the picture.

****

Father Fitz called in the early afternoon. He said he wanted to stop by and give Lily a birthday gift. He had grown close to Auntie Bev and Lily at the nursing home and celebrated Auntie Bev's funeral Mass. That was the first time we met him.

I'm always amazed at the amount and caliber of good that can come from a funeral. There are so many things that would never get said without them. There are people who would never sit in the same room with each other under any other circumstance. And there is always the revival of family stories that might have been forever forgotten. But no other funeral in the history of mankind could have produced more good than Auntie Bev's. It was there that a young woman gained access to a love that for all intents and purposes was eternally lost. It was there that a man, who was at the age when he probably assumed nothing significantly good and new would ever happen to him, was given one of life's greatest gifts.

All Pablo had to do that day was say "Hi Lily," with his soft eyes and sweet smile and stretch out his arms with the familiarity of someone who had embraced her every day of her life. Lily fell right into those arms, weeping over her Auntie Bev, the woman who took care of her all of her life until the tables turned and disabled the able one. Lily was the one that was with Auntie

Bev when she took her last breath. Lily and Pablo said nothing
to each other during the funeral. He sat with his arm around her
and she rested her head on his shoulder, sobbing, sniffling and
blowing her nose on the white handkerchief he took from his
pocket. If Pablo had ever had even a moment of trepidation
about embarking on this venture, it was now dissolved in the torrent of Lily's tears. Three decades of missed time between them,
the dearth of shared experiences and the multitude of unknowns
about the future counted as nothing.

After the funeral, we all went back to the hotel. Pablo and
Lily went for a walk. Jake and my brother Jimmy slouched on a
couch in the sitting area of the suite, watching NASCAR and
eating various varieties of junk food from the vending machine.
Beth, Laura and Katie played video games. Jimmy's wife Georgia had taken their kids outside to play tag in the courtyard. I
joined her, so she would have some adult company. I remember
what it was like standing watch over small children while everyone else was free to converse about something other than
breaking your child of thumb sucking and potty language. Georgia had laid Annabel on a blanket, belly down. The chubby
infant lodged her complaints through grunts and whines and
wrinklings of her face, kicking both legs and punching both arms
into the air simultaneously, hoping to propel her belly across the
blanket to grasp the keys, placed strategically just out of her
reach.

"She's getting her tummy time in," Georgia told me.

"She's so adorable," I said, pulling up a lawn chair next to
Georgia's. Annabel had come out just about dead center, between her father's fair complexion and her mother's dark skin.
She had shiny dark hair, with a soft curl emerging on the very
top. She will probably have curly hair like her mother's. And big
round eyes. Those eyes served as a constant reminder that the
doctors were wrong. Had they been right, she would have had
eyes like Lily's.

"How are you holding up?" Georgia asked, putting her hand
on mine.

"I'm OK," I said, smiling.

"Your aunt was a phenomenal person," she said.

I had never thought of Auntie Bev as phenomenal. She had a good heart. She had raised us well. She fulfilled her duties. But I never would have classified her as phenomenal. My mother, yes. That woman knew how to love. But Auntie Bev kept the trains running, and for that, I am grateful. I am keenly aware that, without Auntie Bev, our lives could have very well been a train wreck after Mom's death.

"We're all going to miss her," I said to Georgia. "I'm going to miss all her wise advice."

"Yeah," Georgia agreed.

"You know, like, should I let my daughter date yet? How much bread crumbs do you put in meatballs? What vitamins should I take when I have PMS?"

"Yes, she always gave good advice. Truthful, honest advice, without sugar coating." Georgia went over and picked up Annabel, who had not yet given up the struggle to fly, or swim or slither, or whatever maneuver she was trying to make. "I think you've had enough tummy time, girly-girl," Georgia said kissing Annabel's fleshy cheek. Georgia sat down and placed the baby on her lap, smoothing out her pink ruffles.

"I owe a great debt to Bev," Georgia said, her face wrinkling into a silent cry.

I hugged and kissed her and told her how much Auntie Bev thought of her. She was so happy the day Jimmy and Georgia got married. Not every woman could have lured Jimmy down the aisle, but Georgia didn't have to. It was Jimmy who did the luring. Georgia may be the only woman on earth Jimmy could have married. He loved his freedom. But he loved her even more. We always said God would have had to create a near-perfect woman for Jimmy to ever settle down. And that's what He did. Because of Georgia's beauty and goodness, Jimmy didn't miss out on all of this, I thought as I watched his children try to out-maneuver each other, shrieking and laughing in the yellow warmth of late summer. Because of Georgia, Jimmy has everything.

I always knew Jimmy would make a good husband. He was always so sweet to Lily, even when we were little. I remember one time, he was sitting next to her in a restaurant booth, stroking her hair, saying "Lily's so pretty. Lily's so pretty." Then he looked at Mom. "Isn't she, Mommy? Isn't she pretty?" Jimmy and I engaged in our fair share of rivalry, but he always coddled Lily. I envisioned him working with disabled people when he grew up. But on Jimmy's twelfth birthday, Jack sent him a 643-part special-edition erector set with a six-volt motor. After he got through building the 25 different models possible with that kit, he began inventing his own contraptions. At the pinnacle of his ingenuity was a series of unrelated items, grouped together to trigger chain reactions. The pencil pushed the marble that descended down the piece of raceway track into the miniature football helmet, which tipped the marble out, which pushed the dominoes, which fell into the toy train car, pushing it into a baseball, which shot onto a clothes pin, which released a string that dumped sand in the truck and moved the seesaw down and pushed the string, which released the straw, which made the spoon knock the marble onto more dominoes, the last of which landed on a fork, which triggered a string that knocked the hammer against the can and spilled the cat food into the bowl. And that is the way Jimmy fed Sunset from that day forward and launched his career as a mechanical engineer. How he got through the math, I'll never know.

****

Aside from Auntie Bev's funeral, the only other time we saw Father Fitz was on Easter. We attended his parish because we haven't gotten involved in our own yet, except for Lily who still goes every week to the church by her group home. People from the young adult group take turns driving her.

After Easter Mass, we drove over to St. Francis Cemetery. Mom and Auntie Bev are buried in the Holy Spirit Garden there. Holidays are soothing times to go. Everyone brings fresh flowers, replacing faded silk ones that adorn the graves year-round. The large mass of the city's greenest grass is dotted with bursts of Easter lilies, pink tulips, daffodils and tiger lilies. The vibrant colors lift your heart into a realm of hope. And then the stuffed bunnies, baskets full of plastic eggs and pinwheels proceed to break it in two. These items are solemn reminders that not all these graves belong to grandparents, that the cycle of life is not always orderly or predictable. It's impossible to fathom, but sometimes people bury their children.

It occurred to me as I watched the cars in the distance, speeding by on the busy road past the cemetery, that there is a whole world of people who have no need to visit a cemetery. Everyone they love is still alive. One day, that will change for every member of the human family, save the ones who die young enough. As for me, it has been a part of my life since I was eight years old.

Mom's death meant a lot more than the absence of a mother. It meant entering an entirely new climate -- like going from Phoenix, Arizona, to Anchorage, Alaska. Auntie Bev always meant well, but it was always clear to us kids that child rearing was not her life-long dream. She had been cajoled into it and you could tell that she wished everyday could have been different.

We brought irises for Mom's grave and hyacinths for Auntie Bev. They were their favorite spring flowers. I always imagine that the souls have a carbon copy in Heaven of whatever anyone brings to their grave. I think about Dia de los Muertos, celebrated in Mexico, when people bring their deceased loved ones' favorite foods to the cemetery. The aroma of the food is thought to reach to Heaven. Under my carbon copy theory, the departed souls would be sitting down to a meal. Could the veil between our world and theirs be sheer enough for flavor to pass through? I was hoping Mom and Auntie Bev would plant these flowers in their garden. That's why I bought potted flowers, instead of ones in vases.

It says something about humanity, that we treat our dead this way. They've made things so peaceful for the dead. The world outside the cemetery walls is loud and harsh for the living. Inside, the birds out-chirp the roar of distant traffic and the far-off sounds of children's voices, taunting their classmates. The dead have the prime piece of sprawling, well-manicured real estate. The posted speed limit is 10 mph. We don't even drive that slowly for living children in school zones. This cemetery is a place set apart, where the crass and brash world of the living is not allowed -- it dare not -- enter in. Across the road in those run-down houses, people are having arguments with their spouses, yelling at their children, holding grudges against their in-laws. But it all halts when one of them is driven through those wrought-iron gates and buried deep within these thirty acres of blessed earth. It's a sad and strange fact. We treat each other better in death than in life.

Except for Lily. There is never any doubt how much she loves you. If the pro-wrestler-caliber hugs are not enough to convince you, there are the dozens and dozens of drawings and notes you stash under your bed in a box marked "Lily."

I know Auntie Bev must have that kind of box full of carbon copies. Lily has written her so many notes and drawn her so many pictures since she died. She got to give them to her today at the cemetery. She traced "Beverly Jean Eagan Greeley" with her finger and then laid herself over the grave marker and cried. "I miss you, Mommy," she whispered. It was one of the few times I'd seen her cry over Auntie Bev since we moved her in with us.

Auntie Bev's life seems so distant now. Her suffering is as if it never were. She braved it all with heroism as her body fell gradually into ruin. I always felt bad for Auntie Bev that she had lost her sense of smell. To me, aroma is one of life's greatest pleasures. I never have invested in a single air freshener or scented candle, though, because the best smells in life are free.

The smell of wet pavement. The papery-plastic smell that fans
your face when a deck of cards is shuffled. The sweet, powdery
scent of clean baby laundry. The aroma of mulled cider simmer-
ing on the stove on a chilly autumn evening. The smell of
winter's first heat coming through the radiator. The smoky aroma of Jake's flannel shirt after a barbeque. The smell of the
summer's first sunscreen. The top of your children's heads. Gar-
denias. Letters from elderly ladies who store their stationary in
cabinets with scented shelf paper. Macy's second floor at
Christmas-time, when the scent of pine and cinnamon potpourri
from house wares mingles with the sachets in intimate apparel.

After paying our respects to Auntie Bev, we reminded Lily
who Mom is, but I think she finds it hard to understand. She
doesn't really remember her at all. Only through pictures and
stories. Childhood is odd. Although it is just a blur in the foggy
recesses of our minds, it forms who we are for the rest of our
lives. I know the love inside Lily is a direct result of Mom's love
for her in the years that lie outside Lily's conscious memory.

"Was I in her belly?" Lily asked, sitting on a concrete bench
near the grave marked Jennifer Anne Eagan, loving mother, Sep-
tember, 12, 1971 - December 24, 2015." Lily twirled a dandelion
she had picked from a crack in the curb near the grave.

"Yes, you were," I said.

"But not in Mommy's belly?"

"No," I said. "She was Mom's sister. That's why Jimmy and
I call her Auntie."

"Like Laura and, and, and Katie and Beth call me Aunt
Lily?"

"Uh-huh."

"Were you in Mama's belly too?"

"No, we were in another lady's belly. But then that lady did
not take good care of us, so Mom adopted us and took care of
us."

"Who is that lady?"

"Her name was Jolene."

"Where she?"

"I don't know."

"Is she dead?"

"I don't know."

Lily watched the dandelion twirling, one way and then another. Then she looked over at me.

"Do you have a baby in your belly?"

"No, I don't, Lily Darling," I said patting my stomach. "Just one too many caramel macchiatos." I had hoped no one had noticed the belly pouch I had developed since becoming a full-time homemaker and having access to the refrigerator and espresso maker all day long.

At this point, I wonder if I will ever return to work again. The timing never seems right for me to start taking on clients. But we're doing OK without my income. Lily's monthly check has helped make it doable. I have never been an at-home Mom before. In some respects, I feel like I missed out on something. I have friends who stayed home with their kids and feel the same way about their foregone career. As someone who has seen both sides, I can assure them, they're not missing much. There's really no way to equate the decision about whether to use welting on the batik with one about whether to let your teenager attend the party down by the river.

"Will you ever have a baby in your belly again?" Lily asked.

"No, Honey," I said.

"Don't you want a baby?"

"Well, even if I did, you can't just order one like a side of slaw," I said, smiling as tenderly as I could. The levity was lost on Lily. She had something pressing on her mind and could not be distracted.

"Will I ever have a baby in my belly?"

"I don't know, Lily. Maybe. Maybe you'll find a special boy and get married and you will have children together."

"Do you think people like me get babies in their bellies?" she asked with the innocent eyes of a small child.

"Some do," I said.

"I really wan- a baby, Tewry. I wan- one in my belly and I wan- one in my heart."

"Twins," I said, putting my arm around her. She instinctively laid her head on my shoulder. "Oh, Lily girl. You have always loved babies."

I felt a deep sadness for her. Lily was a Down Syndrome woman entering her late 30's. The odds of her being fertile during her best years are only 15 to 30 percent. The odds of her finding someone to marry are much slimmer. If she were to marry a man with Down Syndrome, the chances they would become pregnant are pretty much zero. As I wiped a strand of Lily's hair from the corner of her mouth, I blinked tears back into my eyes. I knew she would never have a child of her own, and having three myself, I understand the enormity of that loss, I'm sure, more than she does. Only people who are parents know what people who aren't parents have missed. You can't describe it to anybody. You can't even show them through demonstration.

****

But on the day Lily was turning 37, she seemed to want for nothing, happy to be having another birthday because it meant another birthday party. And not just any ordinary birthday party, but one full of surprises. Lily nearly knocked Father Fitz over when she saw him standing at the door, holding a small box wrapped in white paper with yellow roses. Inside was a Rosary made from olive wood from the Garden of Gethsemane and blessed by the Holy Father on Father Fitz's last trip to the Vatican. Lily pressed it to her face, smiling, and then threw her arms around Father. He gave holy cards of St. Elizabeth, St. Laura, and St. Katherine to the girls, explaining briefly how each became saints. Our children are all named after saints quite by accident. I didn't even know there was a St. Laura until we looked the name up when Laura was preparing for her confirmation. We found out St. Laura, from Spain, lived in the 800s and became a nun after being widowed. She was martyred when the Moors threw her into a vat of molten lead.

But the holy card Father Fitz brought was of a different St. Laura, one from Chile, who was only 12 when she was beaten to death for refusing the advances of the man her mother was sleeping with. Laura's mother had agreed to become the man's mistress in exchange for his putting her daughters through school. Laura feared for the spiritual welfare of her mother and offered her own life to God for her mother's conversion. Laura became ill and her mother had to leave the man to care for her. The man showed up on their doorstep, hoping to molest Laura. She fought him off and he whipped and kicked her and threw her in a ditch. On her death bed, she told her mother she had given her life to bring about her mother's conversion.

"Mama," she said. "I am dying, but I'm happy to offer my life for you. I asked our Lord for this." After Laura's death, her mother left the man, went to confession and became a devout Catholic once again.

Father Fitz agreed to stay for dinner after much cajoling from Lily and me. Lily requested to sit between her Daddy and Father and the three of them played rock, paper, scissors while waiting for the food.

Lily clapped when she saw the basket of French bread. She put two slices of cucumber and a piece of lettuce on her plate when the salad bowl came around to her. She took three wedges of bread. I was not going to nag her about eating her vegetables today. Plus, she would unwittingly consume a few in the lasagna that was the main course. As Pablo and Father explored spiritual matters, doing more talking than eating, Jake ate hearty, going back for seconds and then thirds. Beth sat, staring at her food, pressing her fork down into her Italian sausage, removing it and repeating. Beth had converted to vegetarian about the same time she began experimenting with illicit drugs. She proclaimed that beef was unhealthy, because it had bovine growth hormone. Chicken was unclean, and besides chickens are inhumanely killed. Pork was out of the question because pigs are smarter than dogs and almost as smart as dolphins. Her new favorite foods were fruit smoothies made with wheat grass, with shots of guarana and ginseng -- whatever those are.

"So, what grade are you going into, Beth," Father Fitz asked, chewing his food softly.

"Tenth."

"What school do you go to?"

"Leland."

"Do you like it?"

"It's OK."

"What's your favorite subject?"

"I don't know. English I guess."

"Do you have a good English teacher?"

"Not really."

"A good teacher makes all the difference," he said, smiling at her. She wasn't looking at him. Just at her fork. "I still remember Mrs. Roscoe," he continued as if Beth were interested. "I had her for algebra and it was the first time I ever liked math. She made us laugh. She used to call us gummy bears. I don't know why. And she'd call the unknowns puppies. You know, like, 'OK, Gummy Bears, we're going to solve now for this puppy.'"

"That's what I should name Pablo," Lily exclaimed. "Gummy bear!"

"Did you have a girlfriend?" Katie asked, looking right into Father's face.

"Katie," I protested.

"Nope," he said. "I knew when I was seven that I wanted to be a priest. So I didn't think there was much use in me getting a girlfriend."

"Didn't you go to the prom?" Laura asked.

"Yeah, I did actually. I went with my friend Jill. The boy she liked asked someone else to go, so I took her."

"That was nice of you," said Laura, smiling big at him.

"Well, I don't know," Father said. "She was miserable the whole time, watching him dance with someone else."

Laura and Katie nodded as if they understood.

"Did she ever end up getting the guy she wanted?"

"No," said Father, looking suddenly sad. "She passed away soon after that."

The two younger girls let out a noise that was sort of like a gasp. "How did she die?" Katie asked.

"Car accident," said Father.

Beth had taken her eyes off her fork, which was now perfectly still in her hand, and was looking at Father for the first time.

"That's sad," said Katie. "How old was she?"

"We were 17."

"Did you cry?" Katie asked.

"Oh yes," said Father. "A lot. But, you know, after that tragedy I became even more certain of my vocation." He searched the girls' faces for understanding. "That I wanted to be a priest."

He had stopped eating now. Everyone had, even Jake.

"You know, I guess I realized how short this life is, and that we have to live for something bigger than now. Something eternal. And I really wanted to help people."

It was Father who was the first to resume eating, by picking up his bread and biting at it inattentively.

"So Jake, where did you grow up," Father asked, putting his bread down and propping his head on his hand, elbow on the table.

"Oh, me?" Jake said, swallowing. "I grew up in Minneapolis."

"May I be excused?" Beth asked.

"We're going to have birthday cake, Honey," I said.

"I don't want dessert," she said, picking up her plate and standing up.

"Well, don't you want to sing to Lily?" I asked.

Beth drew a heavy sigh and plopped herself and her plate back down.

"You know," Father Fitz said meticulously wiping each corner of his mouth with the napkin that had been lying in his lap, "in my family we had a tradition of telling our favorite stories about the person celebrating their birthday. Do you have any favorite Lily stories, Beth?"

"I don't know," Beth said. "I can't really think of any right now."

There are certain stories that are stored in the family vault of oral tradition like slide shows relatives subject each other to on holidays and on the days following funerals when the house guests still linger. You never quite know their accuracy. How much is fact and how much is historical fiction or revisionist history? But it's an unspoken rule that each time these stories are told, people who have heard them at every family gathering for decades laugh as if they're just hearing them for the first time.

And so it was when I told my personal favorite about Lily seeing double after eye muscle surgery. Lily looked at Sunset, our cat, and said, "Two Sun-Suns. What's wrong with them?" For two more weeks, while her eyes healed, she referred to Sunset in the plural. "Where they going?" "The Sun-Suns are eating." We knew her vision had returned to normal when Sun-Sun became singular again. And Auntie always said she was relieved that he did because the last thing she needed was two cats with reflux.

"Mom, tell the one about the swim trunks," Katie suggested.

I was considering whether that one would be too embarrassing when Laura emerged from the kitchen, carrying a birthday cake aflame with 37 candles. It was a large sheet cake amassed with gobs of chocolate frosting and dark chocolate shavings of ample size and quantity. In pink script it said, "Happy Birthday, Lily!" and someone with an artistic hand donned the corner with a large white lily. The cake was on the house from the grocery store, where Lily had made friends with the semi-retired woman who runs the bakery on weekends.

After a round of "Happy Birthday," which Lily joined in singing to herself, Father and Jake resumed their small talk about Minneapolis, and then Pablo got Father talking about seminary at the Oblate School of Theology in San Antonio. *That's* the accent I detected. I've heard it said that the Texas drawl is like a communicable disease. It's easy to pick up and, even if you move away, it can stay with you a lifetime, given that there is no known cure. It sounded nice on Father Fitz. Father and Pablo digressed into another deep theological discussion that I can't tell you about because it sounded like a foreign language to me. I don't even know what an oblate is and they have a whole order and a seminary named after it. I haven't exactly been a fallen-away Catholic. I just haven't made faith a priority since Katie received her First Communion three years ago. But after Auntie Bev's funeral, I got to thinking about church again. Thinking about it, but not doing it, but thinking that I should do it. So, it wasn't entirely difficult for Father Fitz, over birthday cake and coffee, to convince me to consider coming to his parish every two weeks to meet with other mothers and study Pope John Paul II's encyclical on the dignity of women.

After cake, Father asked me and Beth to go for a walk. Beth made the excuse of having a stomachache, but Father said the fresh air would do her good. It was almost impossible to say no to the man. Even Beth was cornered by his warmth.

So while Lily challenged Pablo to a game of Crazy 8's, Father, Beth and I walked in the muggy orange dusk. It was one of those days of summer heat waves that occasionally hit Seattle, sending the highs to the 90s and causing sweat to pour from your body like your skin is some kind of sieve. We walked a little while in as close as you can get to suburban silence -- a dog barking far off, the faint shrieks of children swinging, an amateur carpenter pounding away at a cabinet for his garage. Finally, Father spoke.

"Beth," he said. "I would like to tell you something about my past. I hope it won't upset you."

She looked straight at him now, even as we walked.

"My friend Jill was killed by a drunk driver," he said, solemnly.

"That sucks," said Beth looking at the sidewalk in front of her.

"Yeah," Father Fitz said.

We took three more steps.

"That drunk driver was me," he said. "We got drunk after the prom and I drove her home."

Beth was looking down at her feet, which halted for a brief moment and then returned to their regular rhythm.

"I can see you are troubled about many things, Beth," he continued, almost casually. "But, I want you to know that life is good, life is precious. I don't want you to waste another minute of it in misery."

He stopped and took both of her hands in his. "See, there came a moment, long after that tragedy, that I had to make a decision. Do I continue in despair or do I choose to climb out and do something good for someone. I had to decide that it was OK for me to live after my friend died. Not only OK, but required. God was requiring me to go on, not in misery, but in mercy. The alternative would have been the destruction of not one life, but two."

"You're saying that God can forgive anything?" asked Beth.

"Yes. He can and He will."

Her forehead wrinkled slightly as she walked.

"I know it's hard for us to fathom that," Father said. "But whatever is in our past, Beth, we need to confess it, ask forgiveness and leave it there. I am living proof of God's infinite mercy, Beth. Whatever has happened in your life cannot be worse than killing your best friend, can it?"

Beth suddenly had the face of a small child as she looked into Father's eyes. She looked sincere and soulful and even soft -- as if months of ugly scabs, wrought by the wounds of the world, had fallen away.

"You know who would be a great person to help you, Beth?" Father said, softly. "I know she is the kind of woman and he is the kind of man who will listen to you. I know your parents love you no matter what you tell them."

I stood in disbelief at the great gift that was being bestowed on my daughter, on my family. It felt like gold was dropping from the sky and all I needed to do was hold out my hands. I wondered how this man had gleaned all of this insight into Beth from the short time he'd known us. I marveled at his generosity - - revealing his excruciating past to virtual strangers. Who were we to him? Why was he lavishing all this goodness on us? He had come to give Lily a birthday present, and in addition, he was leaving the rest of us with an invaluable gift. And then a sentence flew into my head as if someone else had spoken it: "Where ever Lily goes, goodness is sure to follow."

4

CANDY UNDER THE INCANDESCENT

When we got back home, another card game was underway. Pablo had taught Lily, Laura and Katie to play poker. They were using uncooked Farfalle pasta for money. Father said his good-byes and told me he'd see me next month when I come to the study group. I told him I'd seriously consider it. Pablo folded his hand soon after that and came to help me with the dishes. He took great care, rubbing each glass, inside and out, with the towel, until it looked as sparkly as the ones on the dishwashing detergent commercials.

"You have raised a beautiful family, Terry," he said.

"Thank you, Pablo," I said.

"And it's wonderful what you're doing for Lily."

"We all love her," I said.

"I really wished she could come to L.A.," he said. "But now I think this is the best place for her."

"Well, she has the best of both worlds, as long as you come to visit often," I said, putting my arm around him.

"I would very much love that," he said, squeezing me around the waist.

Laura called out from the card game: "Mom, Katie is cheating."

"I am not," Katie said.

"She looked at Lily's cards," Laura countered.

"I'm not playing anymore," Katie said, tossing her cards in the pot. "This is a dumb game." She ran to the stairs, the part of the house where the most serious protests are voiced and, consequently, the region of our home suffering the most wear.

"You're just a sore loser," Laura yelled after her.

"Laura, that's enough," I said. I cocked my head toward Pablo as we continued to wash and wipe together. "You were saying," I said to him under my breath. "About my beautiful family?"

"Can I have her pasta" Lily said. "Or do you want some, Laura?"

"I think you won the game, Lily," Laura said, folding her cards. "It looks like you have the most pasta."

"Wanna watch TV?" Lily asked, fumbling her cards into an awkward pile. "Daddy, you wanna watch TV?"

"Sure," Pablo said, drying his hands. He folded the towel in exact thirds and hung it on the rack in exact halves. "I will come back and dry the rest later, Mija." He kissed me on the cheek. As he did, a strange combination of sorrow and joy rushed into me and nearly knocked the breath out of me. I don't know why I never contemplated this before, but it wasn't just Lily who missed three decades with this man. It was me too. If Mom and Pablo had married, he would have been my step-dad -- or adoptive dad, or something. I followed him into the family room and sat in the chair-and-a-half, wedged at an angle across from the couch where he and Lily sat.

It's strange thinking how different my life could have turned out for so many various reasons. There are so many alternate realities. I could have been raised by my biological mother, an abusive, neglectful crack addict, but child protective services intervened. I could have been raised by my adoptive mother, but she died. I could have been raised by Pablo, but my adoptive mother never married him. So I was raised by Auntie Bev, and I do wonder what difference that made in who I am. It probably wasn't the best of all the possibilities, but it certainly wasn't the worst. I still miss Mommy, and wish I could have lived my life with her.

"Tell us a story about our mother," I said to Pablo, hoisting my feet into the large chair.

"Ah," he leaned back into the couch, put his arm around Lily, closed his eyes and smiled, as if he were watching the past replay itself on the inside of his eyelids.

"This is my favorite story about Jennifer Eagan," he said finally. "A very poor man came into the newspaper one day with his little son. The man had a very bad toothache, and he was looking for a way to get dental work. The receptionist buzzed your mother because she knew your mother would try to help him. She kept in her address book the number of a dentist and a few doctors who would do work for charity. Anyway, Jen told the receptionist to send the poor man back, so she could give him a phone number. It was only fifteen minutes until deadline, but Jen stopped writing to help him. When Jen saw the little boy, she took a box of granola bars out of her desk and gave them to him. She always kept her desk stocked with food. She loved food. She was a grazer, always eating something. She kept a candy dish on her desk at all times, and people would come by and take a piece of candy and talk to Jen about their troubles, or ask her for her advice on this thing or that thing. She was never too busy to help. It was Brach's that brought her and me together, Terry. Without that candy dish, I would have had no excuse to stop at her desk. I would come by to get a starlight mint or butterscotch disk, but I really wanted just to be in her presence."

"That my favorite," Lily exclaimed, jumping out of her seat. "Butterscotch. I *love* butterscotch."

"Oh, they're good," Pablo said, grinning widely. Lily nestled back into his arm. Pablo leaned his head back again and smiled.

"Jen also kept a lamp on her desk," he said. "She hated florescent lights, and the light from the lamp kind of masked it. That yellow light around her -- it made her seem so warm. But I think even without the lamp, she would have glowed. That was the kind of beauty she had. Something from within."

I nodded. "She always made everything really fun," I said. "She laughed a lot. We laughed a lot."

That's one of the things I really missed after she died. Children who have parents with a sense of humor have no idea how lucky they are. It saddens me that I don't remember that much about life before my mother died. But I do remember *her* -- as vividly as if I had just seen her yesterday. It seemed she had a sense that each day held the potential for being one of those days we would look back on with aching fondness. She had a great love of food and words, the combination of which led to such tasty inventions as Squirbert -- Squirt soda poured over a scoop of rainbow sherbet. For breakfast, there was often Lumpy Cow -- C.O.W. being an acronym for Cream of Wheat -- made lumpy by butterscotch chips.

Pablo, Lily and I talked of food and tradition until around 11, when Lily let out a yawn and Pablo suggested she'd better get some rest. He beamed when she asked him for a good-night kiss. She gave him a peck on the lips and he laid his hand on her forehead and said, "Que duermes con los angelitos, Mija," which means "sleep with the angels," a very nice alternative to "don't let the bed bugs bite."

That night, while Jake snored, I lay awake in bed worrying about the young Father Fitz. I couldn't fathom how a teen boy could hold up. I thought about the mother of that girl for a long time and I wondered if she ever forgave him. I thought about my own girls and realized how crazy it would be to ask that of her. I thought about waking Jake to ask him what he thought about all of this. But I knew what his answer would be: "I don't know, Babe. Stuff happens. People do what they gotta do."

I think I will go to the study group. It will be a good way to meet new people. I am keeping touch with my friends back in Minneapolis, but women need more than e-mail companionship. We need to drink coffee together. And while coffee is certainly not in short supply in this city, people to drink it with are.

I have concocted this rationale for joining the group because the truth seems a bit farfetched. The truth is I am looking for someone to save my daughter, and I figure it just might be the person who is willing to lay bare his soul to a pair of half-opened eyes, weighed down as much by cynicism as by eyeliner. If Beth attends to even a fraction of Father Fitz's past, her future may be spared. We need a family friend like him right now. We may have little, if any, other hope.

****

Yesterday, Lily prepared dinner. She wanted to make it very special for her Daddy. It was his last night here. Lily made meatloaf and mashed potatoes. She knows how to make only five entrees, but she does them well. Her best dish is rice pudding. She also routinely makes hamburgers, baked ziti and sugar cookies, cut into seasonal shapes and decorated with various sizes and colors of sugars. Lily only makes meatloaf on very special occasions. It is a strain for her to get all the ingredients mixed thoroughly through the meat, but she pulled it off, after about a half hour of working it. Pablo was duly impressed and bragged on and on.

"Mijita, I don't think I've ever had a meal this tasty," he said, chewing and cutting more from the hefty slab on his plate. "This is – how do they say? -- exquisite."

"Thank you," said Lily, beaming. "Want some more?"

"Oh, you can bet I will when I finish this," he said. "This is the day you are going to learn, Mijita, that your old man is a pig."

"Wait til you see what for dessert," she said.

"Oh, I can't wait," Pablo said, rubbing his belly. "But I know whatever it is, it can't possibly be as sweet as you."

Lily chuckled as she took a large bite of bread. She still scares us to death with the amount of food she'll put in her mouth at once. But she has survived this long somehow.

Lily added one more thing to her repertoire today, with my assistance. She had asked Pablo what his favorite dessert is and he said blueberry pie. Although it wasn't the most beautiful pie in the world, she did quite well for a beginner, owing to her vast experience with kneading and rolling out cookie dough.

"It gonna rain tomorrow," Lily said. "Can your plane fly in rain?"

"Yeah, it can," Pablo assured her. "Is that what the forecast says? Rain?"

"Yeah. Tomorrow, rain. Day after, no. Next day, yes. Next day, yes."

Lily always knows the five-day forecast. She has a remarkable memory for certain facts. She knows each family member's birthday and their ages. She's great to take along when you go for fast food because she remembers everyone's orders and whether they wanted mustard, ketchup or pickle on their burgers.

"Pablo, have you ever been in a tornado?" Katie asked, taking the napkin from her lap and wiping her fingertips.

"Oh, no, here we go," said Laura, under her breath.

"No, I can't say that I have, Katie," he said, "and I can't say I'm unhappy about that."

Some 10-year-old girls are into Barbie. Many are in to fashion. Most are in to horses. Katie is into natural disasters. Katie loves to watch footage of tornadoes ripping through cities, farms and trailer parks. She likes to try to guess from the footage how it would rate on the Fujita scale. "Oh," she'll exclaim with raised eyebrows. "That one's got to be an F4." She has been trying to convince us to dig a cellar in the back yard "just in case." Unfortunately for Katie, Washington is one of the least likely states in the union for a tornado to hit. Nevertheless, Katie often talks us through the routine of where we should take cover in our house in the event of a twister. She won't admit it, but I think she secretly hopes it will happen. She has a dream of living in tornado alley someday. She wants to be a storm chaser when she grows up. It will be interesting to see what kind of man will marry her.

Already at age 10, she is a rugged, self-assured, optimistic soul who rarely ever finds anything worth crying over.

"You know that lady on the weather?" Lily asked Pablo as he sunk his fork straight down into his second piece of pie.

"Uh-huh," he said.

"I wanna haircut like hers."

"Oh, yeah," he said. "You'd look good in that hair style."

"Can you take me to get my hair cut, Tewry?" Lily asked.

"Sure, we'll make an appointment tomorrow," I said. That will be a great thing to take her mind off of Pablo's departure.

"And I wanna shirt like hers too," Lily added.

"What does it look like?" I asked.

"It's white."

"And what else?"

"It's small. 'Cept for this part." She put her hands on her breasts.

Laughter is like the salt of life. Without it, you can still taste, but the flavors lack clarity and sharpness. Ever since we moved to Seattle, Lily has been our salt. I think I had forgotten, after having been away from Lily for so long, how intense flavors could get.

There is a memory I have of Lily that still brings Jimmy and me to our knees with laughter. Although Lily possesses grace always and everywhere in her spirit, the water might be the only place where Lily possesses it in her physical being, which might be why swimming is one of her greatest passions. Only trouble is, every swimmer has to come out of the water sometime. Even people with good balance feel the abrupt transition between water and land when they first pull themselves out of a pool. You can imagine how Lily -- with her loose hip joints and low muscle tone -- staggers trying to regain her land legs. Given the frequency of her swimming engagements, it was only a matter of time before disaster was going to strike, and on one hazy morning poolside, it did. Lily was getting out of the water, lost her footing on the top step and instinctively grabbed the closest thing within reach, which happened to be the swim trunks of a stranger, who couldn't have guessed when he woke up that morning that he would be bearing his privates at a public pool.

That's the story we told Pablo on the way to the airport this morning. He laughed heartily, put his arm around Lily and said, "Oh, Mija, you'll always be the laughter in my smile." She grinned and rested her head on his shoulder, where it stayed until we pulled into the airport garage. Lily was right about the rain. Jake kept the windshield wipers going for a while after he put the car in park. The droplets were smeared into increasingly subtle streaks while Jake listened to the end of the sports cast. Lily popped her lips and moved index fingers back and forth in unison with the wipers. She has come a long way. I remember as a kid Lily used to scream the whole time the windshield wipers were on. That wouldn't have been such a problem if we had lived in Phoenix. But growing up in Seattle, it was a major quality of life issue for the rest of us, who dreaded going anywhere for fear that our ear drums would burst.

Lily held Pablo's hand all the way to the terminal. Tears streamed down her face as she watched him walk past the doors of the gate and down the jet way. "Bye Daddy, I love you. Bye Daddy. Bye Daddy. I love you. Bye." He walked backwards, waving and throwing her kisses. "Bye, Mija, Love you. Take care of Gummy Bear. I'll see you in a little while."

"It's Pablo," she yelled. "I calling him Pablo. Pablo Puppy."

As he turned out of sight, I wondered if it would only be a little while. I wondered if Lily would see Pablo Perez again at all. Tears stung my eyes and I was surprised at the amount of empathy I felt for Lily. Then, I realized it wasn't empathy. I was sad not just for Lily, but for myself. Sad like I was that late summer day when Jack Greeley packed a half dozen crates into his brand new red Mustang and drove away, leaving us three kids barefoot and waving in our driveway, ignoring the appeals of Auntie Bev to come inside out of the rain. In that moment, I made a silent vow never to get divorced. That's why if there is any leaving to be done, it will be after the youngest of my children is grown.

When Jack's car rounded the corner out of sight, Auntie Bev's commands finally resonated and we realized we were soaking wet.

"That ridiculous car," she murmured, stooped in the foyer to wipe our feet with an old towel. "What kind of idiot buys a convertible in Seattle?"

5

UNUTTERABLE MYSTERY

Father Fitz's study group is run by Lucy Rowley, mother of seven. Her oldest is 10. She wears the youngest in an ample piece of soft linen strapped around her like a very large and bulging Girl Scout sash. I guess she is in her mid-30s. She is very pretty, and her children should count themselves lucky to be sung to sleep by her soothing voice. She is solid and shapely, with a figure I'm sure men would consider sexy in a wholesome kind of way. Her dark hair is blown dry with a roller brush, making soft layers around her face, on which she wears just the right amount of make-up. She looks fresh, even though she has been up every 2 1/2 hours nursing her newborn. She runs a cottage business, custom making baby carriers. She home schools her children.

The four other women in the group are slouches like me. We have two, three or four kids, whom we send off to school. We show up in capri sweat pants, our hair pulled back in thoughtless ponytails. We throw on some lipstick and mascara while stopped in traffic, looking in the rearview mirror. If we hit enough red lights, we will put on eyeliner too. We carry our plastic-lidded paper cups full of coffee with us, sucking down our caffeine like nursing babies, but still looking exhausted.

Lucy passed out the books we would be studying: *Mulieris Dignitatem -- The Dignity of Women,* an encyclical by Pope John

Paul II. When it was my turn to read, I noticed my voice sounded intelligent. My diction was pure and clear, unlike what it sounded like in college, the last time I read out loud in a class.

"People look to the various religions for answers to those profound mysteries of the human condition which, today, even as in olden times, deeply stir the human heart: What is a human being? What is the meaning and purpose of our life? What is goodness and what is sin? What gives rise to our sorrows, and to what intent? Where lies the path to true happiness? What is the truth about death, judgment and retribution beyond the grave? What, finally, is that ultimate and unutterable mystery which engulfs our being, and from which we take our origin and towards which we move?"

I stopped by the parish office after the class to say hello to Father Fitz. He welcomed me with a warm, one-armed hug, extending his arm out straight so as not to spill his coffee on me.

"Terry, I was so happy to see your name on the roster," he said. "So, how did you like the first class?"

"Well, the book seems very intense," I admitted. "But interesting. It's good to connect with other women again. They all seem very nice."

"Yes, it's going to be a good group," he said. He invited me to sit down in the reception area, which was decorated in mission style, with rustic oak and leather chairs. There were two middle-aged women answering phones and doing paperwork at large distressed-wood desks.

"Father, I wanted to thank you," I said, "for talking to Beth the other day. I know it wasn't easy."

"I haven't talked about that incident for quite a while," he said. "It's something I tend to push back to the far reaches of my memory. And only when the Holy Spirit calls it forth, do I recall it."

He took a sip. "Care for a cup of coffee?"

"No thanks," I said. "I had more than my daily quota during that meeting."

He took another drink out of his mug, which had a clipper ship on it. "How about some water?"

"No thanks, I'm fine," I said.

"How's Lily?"

"Great."

"And the kids? Are they all back to school?"

"Yes. They seem to be settling in. But I'm still scared for Beth. I don't know what kind of friends she might end up with."

"Ah, yes. There are few things more valuable to a young person than virtuous friends. I will pray that God sends goodness into her path."

"Thank you, Father." I stood to leave and he walked me out into the parking lot.

"We'll see you in a couple weeks, Terry," he said. Laying his hand on my head and tracing a cross on my forehead, he gave me a blessing. "With the sign of the cross, by passion, death and resurrection of our Lord Jesus, I claim you for Christ."

****

The girls hadn't been home from school for ten minutes before a crisis erupted.

"Mom, why is my painting in the trash?" Beth asked.

"I don't know, Honey. Daddy cleaned the garage yesterday. Maybe he accidentally threw it away."

"No, he didn't," Katie confessed. "I did."

"Thanks a lot, Katie," Beth said. "Now it's ruined."

"Why did you throw away Beth's painting, Katie?" I asked.

"Dad said it was a piece of junk and told me to throw it away," said Katie.

"A piece of junk?" screeched Beth. "I live with a bunch of idiots." She began to storm from the room, but then turned. "Except you, Lily."

She left in a huff, and we didn't hear from her until dinner, at which time she came down and presented Lily with an original piece of art she had apparently produced while sulking in her room.

"Do you like this Lily?" she asked.

"Yes, it pretty."

"I'm glad you like it. I trust your opinion because you're such a good artist."

"Thank you," Lily grinned, putting her arm around her. "But you are better."

"Oh, no," Beth protested. "I could never draw animals the way you do."

"I could never draw people like you do," Lily said.

"Do you know who this is, Lily?" Beth asked.

Lily squinted at it and wrinkled her forehead. Then a huge smile slowly overtook her face. "Daddy!" she exclaimed, picking up the picture.

I stopped stirring and looked at the drawing. Yes, it was quite a good likeness of Pablo Perez sailing a boat.

"Can I keep it?" Lily begged.

"Sure," said Beth. "I made it for you."

"Oh, thank you," said Lily, hugging and kissing Beth. "I gonna hang it up in my room. And I gonna make you a picture too, Beth. For your room."

"Thank you, Lily," said Beth.

"What kin-a animal you wan- me to draw?"

"Surprise me," said Beth.

It was the first of many art barters to come between them. And that's how it happened that Beth's room was transformed into a gallery for Lily's work and Lily's became a gallery for Beth's.

Laura and Lily have their shared art form as well. After dinner, they'll clear the ottoman from the middle of the floor and crank up the disco music. The funniest thing is to watch them do the bump. Lily is always slightly off beat and Laura ends up hitting her at an odd spot, sending her flying off into the sofa. Her laughter zaps all the strength out of her, forcing her to lay there giggling until she can compose herself again and return to the makeshift dance floor.

Katie and Lily share a love of literature. Katie likes to read her own stories to Lily. Today, she read her one she has been working on for quite a while called *Island of the Goats*. From what I can gather, the plot has something to do with a lost civilization of island goat herders, who annihilate themselves through civil war, leaving behind no one but the goats and a 10-year-old boy. A 10-year-old girl is shipwrecked on the island and must try to befriend the savage boy and teach him the ways of peace. It proves to be quite a struggle for the girl, who realizes that taming the boy's violent ways is likely her only hope for survival. She is tempted to despair, until one day, the boy's eldest billy goat begins to talk to her, sharing his sage wisdom and revealing the secret to touching every child's heart.

"That's a good story, Katie," I said from my post at the stove, where I had been intermittently stirring spaghetti sauce nearly all evening. "Why did you choose goats?" I already knew the answer to this.

"Because goats are so cool," Katie said.

Katie has loved goats since she was a toddler. I had often read her a book Mom had read to us called *Beatrice's Goat*. It's based on a true story about a girl in an African village whose life is salvaged when someone donates a goat to her impoverished family, allowing them to sell the goat's milk. Beatrice calls her goat Mugisa, which means "luck." Whenever we would go to the petting zoo, Katie would pick out one goat, give it the name Mugisa, follow it around and pour her affections on it as if it were her very own. Her love of goats was later deepened by several viewings of the movie *Heidi*.

Just as I had gotten the spaghetti and salad on the table, Pablo Puppy came zipping through the kitchen, clenching some highly- prized red, furry object in his teeth.

"Stop that pain-in-the-butt animal!" hollered Laura, following on his heels. "He's got Red Rabbit!"

Pablo Puppy doesn't chew very often, but for some reason, when he does, he chooses from among our home's most sentimental items. Red Rabbit, who holds a pink satin heart between his paws, came into Laura's life when she was 12 years old. I had mentioned to Jimmy on the phone one day that Laura was feeling unattractive and awkward, and a week later, on Valentine's Day, a small package arrived in the mail with Laura's name on it. It was from her secret admirer.

Pablo Puppy crawled under the couch with his catch. Lily got down on her hands and knees and peered under the sofa, derriere in the air.

"Pablo, drop it," she commanded.

And Red Rabbit was saved.

****

Lucy read out loud from *Mulieris Dignitatem* as she bounced her baby on her knee, causing the fat on his ample pink cheeks to jiggle in a very distracting way, so that this one sentence was the only one I heard.

"The history of every human being passes through the threshold of a woman's motherhood."

So true. It is through our mothers that we perceive and interpret reality. I thought about my best friend in high school. Stephanie was the female version of Eddie Haskal, and she spent a lot of time at our house. She was exceedingly polite, with a large inventory of prepackaged compliments. Any doubts about her insincerity were quickly laid to rest one day when she told Auntie Bev how beautiful she looked. Auntie Bev was wearing an old thread-pulled whitish bath robe, a full head of hot curlers and a mint green cucumber facial. This was Stephanie's way of making my Aunt like her.

Her own mother was horrible to her. Trish Herman would sit in her immaculate kitchen, smoking her Virginia Slims at the kitchen island, rarely looking up from her magazine, which I was sure contained quizzes helping you determine how good your sex life is. She was a short woman with bra-length damaged artificially-colored raven-black hair, sharp cheek bones, a small mouth and a peeked nose. Her skin was more leathery than it should have been for a woman in her 30's, and I suspected she was a binge drinker. Her eyes – large and doe-like and framed with a fringe of thick lashes -- could have been pretty enough to redeem her entire face. But they were hot and cruel when they fell on you, and you wished Mrs. Herman would quickly return them to her magazine.

"What's this?" she demanded of her daughter, pointing at a drop of milk on the white Formica.

Stephanie silently got a dish rag and wiped the entire counter, which was already clean, save that one drop of milk.

Mrs. Herman had gotten pregnant and married at the age of 17. She was not in love. She gave birth to a son. Then came Stephanie, the object of her scorn since the day she was born. That, to me, was mysterious, since it was Stephanie's brother who had changed Mrs. Herman's life so drastically. Our working theory was that Stephanie, as a female, represented all that Mrs. Herman had lost. Stephanie had no intention of following in her mother's footsteps. Mrs. Herman thought that Stephanie believed herself to be superior, and she was not mistaken. Stephanie disliked herself, but she loathed her mother. She saw in herself some redeeming qualities, but she saw none in her mother.

Her father was gentle toward Stephanie, but, unfortunately, weak toward his wife. He resigned his home to his wife's tyranny, impotently and silently watching her dote on his son and oppress his daughter. Still, Stephanie loved her father, maybe because a child has to love someone in her own home, and he was the least of three evils. Stephanie couldn't love her brother because he had been indoctrinated into the cruelty of his mother. And so, her pliant and pathetic father was the only choice left. To love and to pity.

Just before our high school graduation, Mrs. Herman had an affair with a carpenter hired to install shelves in the laundry room. Stephanie's father found out and then proceeded to hire him to install cabinets in the garage. Her father was surprised when the carpenter took his down payment and never returned. Mr. Herman had thought the man a trustworthy fellow -- his propensity to sleep with married women notwithstanding.

This is how my best friend grew up, so it was no surprise when she told me that she never wanted children. She went to college, became a high-powered CEO in the information technology industry, married a successful man and devoted her life to the pursuit of wealth. In the ladies' room at class reunions, she would use hushed tones to denounce classmates who had become fat after having "too many" kids. Stephanie's figure was still perfect. She had certainly *not* become her mother. She had made darned certain of that. She had not become a mother at all. And, though I was sad for her, I understood why.

****

I stopped by the parish office after the meeting, but the receptionist said Father Fitz was at a diocesan meeting.

"Would you like me to have him call you?" she asked.

"No, that's OK," I said. "Would you just give him this?"

The thin blonde lady in her 50s took the legal-sized brown envelope from me and put it in a slot behind her marked "Father John Fitzpatrick."

Inside the envelope was a drawing Beth handed me late one night about a week ago.

"Next time you go to your class, can you give this to that priest?" she requested.

She had looked more than her usual tired and unhealthy that night. She looked drained, like someone who had lost a large amount of blood. I would have inquired about her health, but the moment I laid eyes on the drawing, I lost my ability to speak. It knocked the breath right out of me, and I could do nothing but stare at it in silent longing.

****

When I picked Lily up at work, her eyes were red and the purple capillaries under her thin, pale skin were more prominent than usual.

"What's wrong, Lily," I asked. "Why have you been crying?"

"That mean man say I smash his bread," she said, rubbing her eyes.

"Did you?"

"No, never smash his bread. He say I do, but I don- smash his bread. Mr. McCrae say I can't bag that mean man's groceries. He say Mark has to. That mean man yell at me. But I don-smash his bread."

Lily's speech suffers especially when she is upset. I remember how Auntie Bev used to arrive at her wit's end trying to figure out what Lily was saying through her tears.

"Ai, eh, eh, ee, ooh, uh, ai," Lily would blubber on.

"That was a lot of verbs -- almost all of them, in fact," Auntie Bev would reply. "Try some consonants and see if someone might be able to understand you."

I patted Lily on the shoulder, trying to imagine what kind of human being would value a loaf of bread so highly as to hurt the feelings of a sweet, lovable woman with Down Syndrome.

"It's OK, Lily," I said. "I'm sure Mr. McCrae knows you didn't smash his bread. No other customers ever complain, right?"

"Right," she said. "I don- smash that man's bread. I don-smash anyone's bread. I like doing a good job. I like making people happy. That mean man is not happy. But I don- smash his bread."

"I know," I said. "He's probably just a miserable old man, who never had enough people be nice to him in his life."

"Mr. McCrae say he not mad at me. He say I do a good job and make people happy."

"Well, you certainly make me happy," I said.

She gave me a wide smile. "I don- smash your bread."

"No," I said. "And you give me many, many other reasons to be happy."

"I don- break your eggs."

"Yes, that's true," I said. "But that's not why I love you."

She was quiet for a minute and then said, "Tewry, I sorry for eating your science egg."

I can't believe she still remembers that horrible day.

When we got home, Laura and Beth were at it again -- this time over a long-sleeved black lace shirt.

"She gave it to me," Laura said, "and now she's saying she didn't, and I want to wear it to the mall."

"When are you going to the mall?"

"After dinner," Laura said. Then she remembered who she was barking orders to. "Can I?"

"Do you have homework?"

"Done."

"Beth, Honey, can she wear it tonight? She'll give it back to you tomorrow."

"I was going to wear it tonight," Beth said.

"And where are you going?" I asked.

"Out with my friends."

"Honey, 'out' is not a location. It's a preposition."

Beth rolled her eyes. "I need my shirt back."

"Where are you going tonight?" I pressed.

"Movies. I need my shirt back."

"Did you give it to Laura?"

"Yes," Laura said.

"Beth? Did you?" I asked.

"Yes, but I need it back now."

Jake came down from his office and headed for the pantry.

"Hey girls," he said.

"Beth, it's not nice to take stuff back once you give it to someone," I said. "You're going to have to let Laura wear it. But you can borrow it from her another day."

"Borrow my own shirt," Beth huffed. "Now I've heard everything. She always gets whatever she wants because she's special."

"That's not true," I said indignantly.

"That's right," Jake piped in. "Laura is *not* special and don't ever say that about your sister again."

Beth looked at her father and rolled her eyes and then smirked ever so slightly. Somewhere under that world-weary veneer, she still loves her Daddy.

"Anybody for volleyball?" Jake asked, crunching a fist full of potato chips. "I have twenty minutes until my next conference call."

"Me!" Lily yelled, trotting for the back door.

"It's raining, Daddy," Katie pointed out, without looking up from her *Eyewitness* book. "Mom, did you know only one in four lion cubs survive to adulthood because hyenas and leopards and other pred-"

"Mom, did you buy Activia?" Laura was holding the fridge door open standing erect, looking straight ahead into the fridge, the same way all members of the household look for things in there. That's the reason only the mother can find anything. No one else but her will bend a knee to find anything in the bottom drawer or stand on tiptoe to see clear to the back of the top shelf. A mother knows it's all about viewing angles, so she will even bend over with her butt sticking out of the fridge, if that's what it takes. Everyone else in the family, they just stand and gaze and ask.

"On the second shelf," I said.

"Oh, it's only a drizzle," Jake said. "Zip your jacket, Lily."

"Anyways," Katie continued, "The cubs stay in like a day-care with their aunts and other lionesses who take turns taking care--"

"I don't see it," Laura said.

Katie has never been able to get a complete thought out of her mouth. But it's her own fault, really The child crafts the world's longest sentences, filled with detail that interests no one

64

in the world but her. Lily is the only one who can sit quietly and listen to Katie until she's through. Lily appreciates Katie's animated style of story-telling as well as her depth of knowledge on so many topics, owing to Katie's insatiable hunger for the written word. She will read anything. Weather reports, office supply catalogs, blender directions.

"And did you know a lion's roar can be heard up to five miles away and male lions recognize each other by the smell of their urine. What's urine? Is that pee?"

"Yes," I said.

"I still don't see it," Laura said, still standing, gazing.

"I'll get it," I sighed. A volleyball hit the window. The rain was coming down pretty good and Lily had fallen in the mud already. For a second, I saw her at age 8 or 9, playing in Auntie Bev's back yard. We spent a lot of time wet when we were kids -- playing slip and slide, running through the sprinklers, waging hose fights. I would hold Jimmy down so Lily could squirt him. It was amazing the trajectory she got on that hose. Meanwhile, Auntie Bev would be hollering about the windows getting inadvertently sprayed.

"Who taught that child to put her finger inside the hose?" she'd ask.

About every three minutes or so, someone would wipe out on the slip and slide. Because I was the biggest, it would usually be me. I'd run out of track and go skidding onto the grass, elbows first. I'd lie there wincing in pain. Jimmy would be yelling at me to get my butt out of the way because it was his turn. It was during those times that Auntie Bev instilled in us the virtue of compassion.

"Show some empathy and hose her down," she'd shout at Jimmy.

That's the kind of home we grew up in. Tough and humorous many times. Tough and humorless others.

We all grew skilled at dealing with both. Lily was especially good at it. Any time Auntie Bev chewed someone out, Lily saw it as her role -- maybe even her calling -- to restore peace to the family. She would don her sweetest smile, whisper a breathless "hi," hug Auntie's leg and kiss her hand. Even if Auntie never uttered a word, Lily had a knack for picking up on nonverbal hostilities and she would quickly go to work to appease impending vengeance with her mood-altering affections. Sometimes it worked.

6

MERCY DRAWN

Today, I had the third meeting of my Moms' group. Irene, a mother of two, broke down in tears. Her yearning for more children tormented her. Her husband had undergone a vasectomy years ago. She has dreams about the babies she never had. Her two children have begged her to have more kids. She feels she has cheated them out of the one thing that only she can give them -- siblings. One of the women suggested adoption. The other mentioned a vasectomy reversal. I have never heard of such a thing. Or, if I have, I've never paid it any attention. I understand Irene's regret. I have to say that something changed between me and Jake after he had his vasectomy. I can't put my finger on it, but there was lost magic. I guess there's a bit of a thrill every time you make love, thinking you might be making a baby. Not that I necessarily want another baby. But there's something whole and wholesome about knowing we two people could do something together that no other two people can do. No one else can conceive the specific child that we could. And that particular child that can be conceived in that particular moment is like no other child that can ever be conceived again or has ever been conceived in the past. Once that moment is gone, so too is the possibility of that human being.

Unlike in Irene's case, the vasectomy was my idea. I had suggested it because having another baby would have prolonged my plans to leave once the kids were grown. I didn't want to set us back any more time.

I had planned to stop off at the grocery store on my way home, but all I really needed was eggs and milk. I was so exhausted, I decided to go straight home and take a nap and just grab a few groceries later when I pick up Lily from work. I needed a house all to myself before the kids got out of school. When they are home, they have me bouncing around like a pinball. If there's a moment when I manage to escape the forces of inertia and sit down somewhere, I'm viewed as fair game for a round of chess or tic tac toe or teen-aged manipulation. It's just nice to have a space without anyone else in it once in a while. Katie is one of those sticky people. She can't live comfortably without having some part of herself in contact with some part of you. It's like she is charged with static cling. Although she weighs seventy-two pounds, she still likes to sit in my lap. There is a bright side to that, though. I always know where she is. Unlike Beth, who stayed out until 11:30 last night and never called to tell me where she was. She claims she was out on the beach, drawing. When I asked to see her artwork, she said she wasn't done with it. When I asked her where her flashlight was, she said she didn't need one because there was a full moon. She looked tired, but not stoned, really. Although I wouldn't consider myself an expert at detecting drug use. If I was, my daughter couldn't have evolved, unnoticed, into the mess she is.

Beth has always been one to try new things, unless of course they are slimy, so the fact that she has experimented with drugs is not surprising. Even as a kid, she was always looking for a new flavor of ice cream. Laura always orders chocolate. Katie always orders chocolate chip cookie dough, much to the disgust of the rest of her family. Nothing wrong with cookie dough in ice cream, really, because anything surrounded by ice cream is palatable. It's just Katie's technique. She spits the blobs of cookie dough out in a pile on one side of her bowl and saves them until the ice cream is gone, rolls them into one big ball and takes small bites until it's finally -- and thankfully -- consumed. Watching that will kill any craving for cookie dough if one ever existed. It's a gross habit, but I will gladly take it over all the other dysfunctions we are dealing with.

Beth's psychiatrist put her on anti-depressant medication a few weeks ago. The doctor said puberty probably triggered the onset of clinical depression, and Beth's experimentation with illicit drugs is a way of trying to medicate herself. She also told me progress in treating the underlying problem might be very slow because Beth is holding back. There is something she is refusing to address. The doctor asked me if I might know what it is. I wish I did, but she holds back from me too. I fear the deep pain she suffers has something to do with me or my parenting. The psychiatrist assured me that's the conclusion all parents jump to, often unnecessarily.

I was not shocked to learn that there is a chemical imbalance in Beth's brain. I was, however, shocked to learn of the psychiatrist's other finding. Beth has no idea that our love for her is unconditional. The counselor said that's not unusual. Very few children, she said, know that there is nothing they can do to lose their parents' love. It's something that is rarely verbalized because parents feel it so strongly, they assume children know it. In fact, the messages that often are verbalized tell children the opposite. "You did such a good job on that. I love you so much." or "You are so funny. I just love you." Those are the words that link love with an action, skill or attribute.

When I told Father Fitz what the counselor had said, he was not surprised.

"Even adults – or maybe I should say *especially* adults -- have a difficult time with the concept of unconditional love," he said. "They know they have it for their children, but they can't fathom that anyone would have it for them. This is why the love of God, portrayed through the story of the Prodigal Son, seems so radical."

Father took me by the arm and looked deep into my eyes.

"Terry, I feel I need to impress on you the danger that Beth is in."

"I know. I'm just glad she's on medication now. Maybe that will keep her from turning to drugs."

"It's not the drugs that pose the greatest risk to her, Terry. The greatest danger comes from deep within. She is harboring something very destructive. I don't mean to scare you, Terry, but you've got to find a way to reach her. I fear you could lose her.

"Lose her?"

"Children can very quickly fall into despair, Terry. And then it's very dangerous."

I knew what he was saying without saying it. My heart pounded hard. "How do I reach her?"

"Your knees have to hit the ground. Pray for a way to let Beth know you love her no matter what. That she can tell you anything and everything. Having a mother like that saved my life."

****

Lily was waiting out front on a bench when I pulled into the grocery parking lot 10 minutes early. When she saw our car, she picked up her lunch box and ambled to the curb. I decided just to skip the milk and eggs.

"Hey, Lily, how was your day?"

"OK," she said. Her head was hanging and she answered much softer than usual, as she climbed into the car.

"Anything new?" I inquired, putting the car in drive.

"Mr. McCrae said I can- come to work anymore."

"What?"

"Not this week. Not 'til Monday."

"Why?"

"I ate the Snickers."

"What Snickers?"

"The one the person didn- take."

"What do you mean?"

70

"I forgot to put the Snickers in the bag. The lady bought it and I forgot to put it in."

"So you ate it?"

"Yeah. I love Snickers."

"But someone else paid for it."

"Yeah, the lady."

"Then why did you eat it."

"She didn- take it home with her."

"Yeah, because you forgot to put it in the bag. That was your job to make sure it got into her bag."

"That what Mr. McCrae said. He very sad with me."

"Oh, Lily," I said, half scolding and half sympathetic. "What is the policy for food that the baggers forget to bag?"

"Polishy?"

"Yeah. What should you do with the food you forget to put in the bag?"

"Save it at customer service," she said.

"So, why did you eat it?"

"I love Snickers."

Two day's suspension seems kind of brutal for an employee with Down Syndrome and an insatiable sweet tooth, I thought.

"But everyone was counting on you to put it in the bag, not eat it. You should have just bought yourself a Snickers. Now you got yourself suspended and you're going to lose two days' pay, instead of 80 cents for a Snickers bar. That was a very expensive Snickers bar you ate."

"But yummy," she said.

"Oh Lily."

"You mad at me too," said Lily, hanging her head.

"Well, everyone makes mistakes," I said. "We just have to learn from them and don't make them again. Just make it a point never to make the same mistake twice."

"No, I don- do it twice. The other time, I ate Hostesh cupcakes. They yummy too."

"Lily!" I said. "That wasn't the first time?"

"Yeah, I never eat Snickers before."

"You're not supposed to eat any food that someone else paid for, Lily. If you keep doing that, Mr. McCrae will think you're forgetting to put it in the bag on purpose, just so you can eat it. That's stealing."

"No, no, no, no, no," she said, shaking her head. "I don-steal!"

"Well, I know you don't, Lily, but that's what it looks like. You must never eat someone else's groceries, OK?"

"I know," she said. "I tell Mr. McCrae I wo- do it again."

Bagging groceries is the perfect job for Lily. She has always loved the grocery store. And what's not to love for someone who has such a passion for food? It's the equivalent of an animal lover going to the zoo. When we were kids, I remember it being almost impossible to get Lily out of Safeway.

One time Auntie asked me to put some strawberries back in the produce aisle while she finished checking out. She had found a better deal on the bigger batch, but had forgotten to put away the small one. Knowing that checking out meant it was time to leave, Lily came with me, but decided, instead of returning to Auntie Bev, she would embark on an expedition through the store, trailing a very agitated sister behind her. When I caught up with her and tried to pull her back to the check-out area, she sat down in the middle of the canned vegetable aisle and refused to budge. She'd still be there today if a very nice lady hadn't introduced herself as "Anne" and told Lily she wanted to meet her Mom, and could she please lead the way to her. Auntie thanked the woman profusely. Anne told her she has an aunt with Down Syndrome.

"Very sweet, but very stubborn," the woman said.

"You got that right," Auntie told her with a wink and a smile. I think at that moment it became clear to all of us that this problem with Lily was not short term. And yet, when I think of how far she's come, it astounds me. It's been many years since I've knocked over a Cap'n Crunch display or White Cloud toilet paper end cap trying to put Lily in a half-nelson.

Now we just have to keep her away from other people's candy bars.

"Can I go to Confession?" Lily asked, grabbing my arm, which I had to stiffen to keep from veering out of my lane.

"Confession?"

"I wanna tell God I sorry."

"Sorry for what?"

"I ate the Snickers bar. And the cupcake."

"Oh, Lily, I'm sure those aren't sins you need to confess."

"That not my Snicker bar and I ate it. That not my cupcake and I ate it. Just like I ate your science egg."

"But you didn't mean any harm, Lily. You don't need to go to Confession for those kinds of things."

"I wanna go. Will you drive me? Please?"

"OK," I said. "We'll go Saturday."

"No, not Saturday," she said. "Right now. I wanna see Father Fitz right now. He always tell me God forgive me. That make my heart happy."

"Well, he probably isn't even there right now, Lily. Confessions are on Saturdays."

"I don- wanna wait," she said. "Please drive there now."

It was such a beautiful afternoon that, while Lily was in the confessional, I waited out in the courtyard. I watched a bee buzz around a basket of silk flowers suspended from a wrought iron plant hanger high on the bell tower. The bee would start to land and then change its mind, hover over another flower for awhile and then consider landing again. It never did sit. I felt sorry for it. I imagined how confused it must be. The flowers were so beautiful, but where was the nectar? There was nothing life-giving or life-sustaining about them. Their whole purpose was for appearances. What did beauty matter to a bee? And suddenly, I understood, somewhere inside too deep for words, what had happened between me and Jake.

Lily and Father Fitz came strolling out into the courtyard arm-in-arm. Lily was beaming.

"Terry, I can't tell you how moved I was by Beth's picture."

"It was amazing," I said.

"I am very touched that she wanted me to have it," he said. "It is really profoundly insightful. Do you have a minute? Come with me."

Father showed us to his office, where Beth's drawing was framed and sitting next to the warm glow of a desk lamp on his credenza beneath a large crucifix, which took up much of the wall behind it.

"Beth will be honored that you liked it enough to have it framed" I said. I walked around his desk to get a better look at the drawing. A kneeling teenage boy weeps over the body of a pretty young girl, laid out in the street beside a mangled car. A hand rests on the boy's shoulder. The hand has a wound in the palm.

I still can't believe my Beth could have drawn something like this. It isn't so much the artistic talent that floors me as it is its poignant empathy. Beth stepped outside her own misery to portray the glimmer of hope in someone else's.

"You'll need to bring her in and show her where I put it," Father Fitz said.

"Beth and me great artists," Lily said. "I have Beth drawings in my room too."

"You are very blessed," Father told her. "And Beth is very blessed, too, to have your artwork."

"I wanna go pray in the chapel. Can I go, Tewry?"

"For a minute," I said.

"Yay!" she said, running out the door.

"I'll meet you in there," I called after her.

Father picked up a white envelope from the desk and handed it to me. It said "For Beth" in blue cursive.

"Would you give this to Beth for me? Please feel free to read it first, Terry. It's a story I'd like to share with you, too."

"OK, thanks."

"It was so good to see you and Lily today. I'm glad you came by."

"Well, Lily insisted. I guess her conscience was really bothering her."

"She is a pure and lovely soul. You know, I can hear your confession too, if you'd like. I really have nothing on my schedule right now, which is quite strange, I must say."

I was not prepared, but I could find no words within me to decline such an offer. And so, I told my sins to a priest for the first time since Katie's First Reconciliation three years ago. This time, I had the knowledge and the courage to include all of my sins.

I found Lily hunched over with her forehead on the plush berry-red carpet of the chapel. I knelt beside her to pray my penance.

As soon as we left the church parking lot, I pulled into a residential area and parked in front of a stranger's house.

"Why we here?" Lily asked. "Are we going to a friend house?"

"No," I said. "I just need a minute to read this letter from Father."

"Can I listen to music?" she asked, reaching for the knob.

Here Comes the Sun streamed into my ears, as I unfolded the plain white paper, which smelled like the inside of Father's office – a comforting combination of coffee and French vanilla air freshener. I thought I might have detected a hint of incense like they burn at church, too.

"Dear Beth,

Last week, I travelled to my native Portland to see a woman who is dying. I hadn't seen her in eighteen years, and she didn't remember me. I had to remind her that I was the one who was responsible for her daughter's death. That I had once asked for her forgiveness and she was unable to give it. I told her that I would ask one more time, in hopes that our souls could both be set free. Then I showed her your drawing. She broke down crying, then so did I. We held onto each other for a long time and then she said the three words I've longed to hear for nearly two decades. "I forgive you." She asked me to hear her confession and I anointed her. Both of us received spiritual healing that day. It was as valuable to her soul to offer me forgiveness as it was for my soul to receive it. Even more so, actually.

I wanted to tell you, Beth, how crucial your life is in God's plan. If our paths hadn't crossed, and I hadn't told you about my past, and you hadn't made that drawing, I don't know if I would have thought to try again to ask for that woman's forgiveness. You played a key role in bringing peace to someone's soul. God has many more of those plans in store for your life.

I can't tell you how much I love the drawing. It touched me very deeply. I see that you are a very insightful soul. It is often those souls who feel the most deeply, who are the most troubled. Sometimes these are the souls who look for ways to alleviate the pain. There is only one way to treat the pain with any lasting efficacy. Only the Divine Healer, can safely and permanently take away our pain. He alone knows the full extent of our suffering, for He too endured the full spectrum of human suffering. That is the Truth your drawing captures so beautifully. And it is the Truth I will remember every time I think of you.

Warmest Regards,
Father Fitz

"You know, Beth," I told her after she read the letter, folded it and silently returned it to the envelope, "I can't imagine my life without you."

"Really? I can. I can imagine your life having a lot less trouble without me."

I pushed a mound of dirty clothes to the end of the bed, clearing a spot for me to sit next to the stranger who, at one time, not so long ago, had resided in my womb. I wrapped my arms around her. She sat limp.

"The world would not be the same without you, Beth. It would be sadder and darker. We would all be poorer. We treasure you."

"Who is we?"

"Your Dad and me. Your sisters. We all love you. No matter what you've ever done or what you'll ever do, we love you. Father Fitz loves you too. Can't you tell from the letter what a difference even just one day in your life made?"

She stared at the envelope in her hand.

"What ever your problems are, Honey, we can help you," I said. "We will all be there for you. You don't have to be afraid of losing our love, no matter what you tell us."

She shifted her shoulders to break my embrace. "I need to go to the bathroom."

"Father Fitz, he's good to talk to too, Beth." I told her as she left the room. "I talk to him about my problems all the time. He's a good listener. And I always feel a lot better."

"I'll keep that in mind," she said, shutting the bathroom door.

7

SOMETHING RADICAL

I wanted to do a little research before I presented Jake with my newest request. It seemed like I was always asking him for things. Not little things, like hanging up a shelf or fixing a baseboard. I had long ago decided not to be one of those nagging wives with the honey-do lists when I myself am more than capable of pounding a nail into a wall. But I have asked and received very large gifts from Jake, like vasectomies and relocations halfway across the country. Now I was preparing to ask him for another one. I googled and came up with a website displaying a photo of a rodeo cowboy riding a bull, with the caption that read as follows:

If you're worried about how you might feel after your reversal, just ask our patients. Just two weeks after his reversal, Pro Rodeo Bull Rider Tommy Gomez was back on the job!

The ad went on to explain that an estimated 40,000 men each year change their minds about their vasectomies and seek a reversal to restore their fertility. It called the three-hour out-patient micro-surgery one of the most tedious in all of medicine.

"Who knew? It had been such a minute movement -- the snip necessary to end the possibility of new life. Yet it requires such great skill to restore it.

Although our health insurance covered the vasectomy, I called and learned it does not cover a reversal. The timing for presenting this to Jake will be delicate, like the surgery, which, according to the website, is done under a microscope, using sutures finer than a human hair. To make my best pitch, I decided I should try to beguile him with my charms in the middle of the day, when all the kids are away at school and Lily is at work. Put on my black silk night gown and make a nice brunch. Hey, it worked for Queen Esther, the biblical heroine who planned a feast for her husband, the king, to save her people from death by the King's decree. The only problem is, like Esther, I keep chickening out. And unlike Esther, I don't have an Uncle Mordecai to kick my butt until I get it done. So, while I've already succeeded in pulling off three very enjoyable daylight seductions, I still haven't found the courage to ask Jake for the desire of my heart.

****

I was rummaging through the attic today, looking for my box of color samples. We've gotten around to redecorating pretty much the entire house, except for the basement. I want to turn it into a home theater and game room. I couldn't find my samples, but I did find a box marked "For Bev." I immediately recognized it as Mom's handwriting. Jake had three boxes of Auntie Bev's belongings shipped to us in Minneapolis after she died. We put them in the attic, intending to sort through them later, and then moved them, still sealed with their original tape, to our new attic in Seattle. I opened the one Mom wrote on. Inside was a picture of my grandparents, Mom and Auntie Bev at the beach -- the perfect family of four, slightly sunburned and covered in sand. I held it for quite a while, thinking about a similar picture of the five of us on a beach vacation when I was a kid. It was right after that trip to Vancouver's Kitsilano Beach that Jack left us. I was 11 years old and I took it personally. Eleven-year-old girls take everything personally.

The thing we loved about Kitsilano Beach is that it had a huge swimming pool, so you could swim in the heated water while looking out over the ocean, without the inconvenience of pesky seaweed, dangerous undertows or ominous ocean creatures. It was even purified with salt instead of chlorine. It was there, as Jack struggled to keep a watchful eye on Lily in Canada's longest pool, that we all realized Lily had a gift. Auntie Bev signed her up for Special Olympics soon after we returned.

I laid the photograph of Mom and Auntie Bev's beach trip on a stack of old books so I could remember to bring it down and show Lily and the girls. Then I unpacked a high school yearbook, an unfinished manuscript for a novel Mom was writing and a Bible with her handwriting in the margins. I pulled something wrapped in newspaper from the bottom corner of the box. It was a paperweight -- the kind with a clear glass dome into which you can insert a photo. The picture inside was of a young woman, head tipped back away from the camera, eyes pointed toward it. If you strained you could consider her half smiling. If it wasn't for the undercurrent of melancholic disenchantment harbored beneath her smirk, I could have been staring square-on at a photo of my Laura. I turned the paperweight over. Someone had written in silver ink on the black velvet: "Jolene 2006." Jolene was my birthmother. I decided to pass it on to Laura. It was perfect for her, not only because it contained her genetic legacy, but also because Laura is in desperate need of a paper weight. She has an unnatural affinity for her ceiling fan, which scatters her papers to the four corners. Laura loves the cold. She doesn't love *being* cold. She loves being warm in the cold. Which explains why she wants the fan on in her room year round. This enables her to wear flannel pajamas and pile on blankets for as long as possible into the spring.

I wish I could give Laura a lovelier picture of her grandmother. The paperweight photo shows a beautiful young woman. But she is not lovely. Jolene's vacant eyes haunt me. I identify a bit too much with them these days. Something strange happened to me several years ago. All of a sudden, one day I realized, I couldn't conjure up any feelings of warmth toward my husband or children. Sometimes I'd be peeling carrots or stirring pudding, watching them play -- all four of them rolling around wrestling on the family room floor -- and I would be thinking I ought to feel something for these people. It was disturbing to realize I could no longer recognize any cuteness or beauty in them, so I pacified myself with inane distractions, like "I should have bought a two-inch shag instead of a berber. It would have made for more comfortable wrestling." I filled my head with trivial matters so I wouldn't go off into something deep like "Maybe if I could fall in love again with somebody, I would relearn how to feel."

I decided to take my own advice – the piece I had given Beth – and confide in Father Fitz. "When I look at my children or my husband, it is as if I am looking at a brick wall," I told him after the moms' meeting. "And everything I do for them is out of a sense of obligation, not love."

"Not a *feeling* of love, but out of love nonetheless," he said, nodding.

"What do you mean?"

"Love is sacrifice. It means doing things that you don't feel like doing. So fulfilling your obligation actually *is* love."

"But, don't you think there's something wrong when it's hard to say 'I love you' to your own children and husband? I have to force the words out."

"Love is more about doing than saying or feeling. It's wanting the best for the other and doing everything you can to ensure it. It's the self-sacrificing love the Greeks called *agape*. And the fact that you force the words out shows you want your children to feel loved, which proves that you do indeed love them."

"Hmmmm," I said. "I'm going to have to think about that one for awhile."

"Let me ask you, Terry," Father said. "How do you feel towards God?"

"The same as toward my family. Nothing. I don't even want to pray any more. I don't really talk to God like I used to. He doesn't even seem real to me anymore, even though I know that He is."

"Ah," Father said, nodding. "The dark night of the soul."

"Wow," I said. "You've got a name for everything."

Father's chuckle spilled a spreading warmth into the room.

"Well, it's not my description. I'm not nearly deep enough to come up with that one. That's how saints describe the arid period a soul goes through when prayer seems to do nothing for it. There is great temptation to quit praying during this period devoid of consolations -- or what we would call warm and fuzzy feelings. But the soul that perseveres in prayer through those times proves itself well tested and forges an even stronger spiritual life, and reaches an even higher level -- and ultimately -- union with God."

"And what if you haven't persevered?"

"Never too late," he said. "You know, many people tell me they're suffering a mid-life crisis. Life needs to mean something and they know theirs somehow does. But what? If they were single, they could go do something radical to answer that question. Like join the Peace Corp. But as a wife and mother -- or husband and father -- with so many responsibilities, doing anything radical would be irresponsible."

"Uh-huh," I nodded.

"Oh, but not true."

"Not true?" I said.

"Not true," he confirmed. "You want to do something radical?"

"Like what?"

He reached into his shirt pocket and handed me a scrap of paper. "Here. Here's a woman with a premature baby. Tell her Father Fitz sent you from Queen of Peace to pray with her."

I looked at the white scrap, which had been ripped off a larger piece of paper. *Nina Robinson. Harborview Medical NICU.*

"Her baby was born at 25 weeks gestation," Father said. "She's a pound and half. They're not sure she's going to make it. I baptized her yesterday. Little Sophia."

"I just pray with her?"

"Pray hard."

I slid the scrap of paper into the outside pocket of my purse. "How's Beth doing?"

"I can't get through to her, Father. It's like she's built a fortress against everyone who cares about her. Her father has been taking her to play basketball every Saturday morning, and he's lucky to get two words out of her. I offer to take her shopping or out to eat, she comes up with excuses why she can't or why she has to cut it short. "

"She's smart. She knows what you're up to. But you can't give up. You've got to find a way. You've got to, Terry."

"It's just so hard to guage what's going on. We get no feedback at all from her."

"When you see tears, you'll know change has become possible."

"How do we do it, Father? How do we reach her?"

"I wish I could tell you how, Terry. But only God knows that. Remember what I said about your knees. It's where parenting begins."

On the way home, I kept trying to work out why a priest would send a woman who says she doesn't pray to keep vigil with someone who is in desperate need of prayer. I should have asked Father what prayers to say. The only thing that came to mind was the Rosary. I was certainly no good at spontaneous prayers. I wasn't good at the other kind either. I haven't prayed a Rosary since I was on a retreat in high school, but I remembered I had one in my drawer that used to be Auntie Bev's. When I got home, I slid my hand to the bottom of my nightgown drawer and pulled out the red glass beads linked with gold. It was heavier than I remembered as I picked it up and let each bead fall one at a time into my palm. The sight of it brought me back to the one and only time I ever saw Auntie Bev holding a rosary. It was at Lily's bedside, when she had been hit by the bus. It was this very rosary that Auntie Bev clenched in her trembling hand. I wondered how she came to possess it. Someone must have given it to her. She would not have bought it.

A nurse outside the neonatal intensive care unit showed me how to scrub up. I rubbed amber-colored disinfecting soap onto my hands and lower arms, up to my elbows, and pressed the foot pedal under the enormous stainless steel sink, watching the torrent of water rush over my hands and blast off the germs, which ended up, I assumed in the mound of bubbles forming at the drain. Father Fitz must have gone through this same hand-washing ritual yesterday. I thought about his large hands pouring holy water over a tiny baby's head. I wondered how it would be possible for that baby to die now, after having been touched by him. A knot was growing in the pit of my stomach. I had no idea what I was about to see or how I would handle it.

I was allowed in only because Nina Robinson told the nurses that I was a friend of hers, a status she immediately granted, solely on the basis that Father had sent me. The nurse explained that the ward we were about to enter is for micro-preemies, those whose birth weights were less than 1 3/4 pounds. I didn't even know there was such a thing as a human being that small. Rows of babies lay naked down to their diapers in plastic boxes they call isolettes -- incubators necessary to keep the babies warm, since their own body regulators aren't finished developing. A lot of things aren't finished at 23, 24, 25 weeks gestation. But one thing is: the hypnotizing effect that all hu-mans possess when they're fresh out of the womb. Thankfully, it isn't rude to stare at a newborn. But even if it were, I wouldn't have been able to help myself. I don't know how I got my eyes off of a baby and onto a memo board, but I think I might have audibly gasped when I saw "Birth weight: 13 oz; Today's weight: 16 oz. written in blue marker. Thirteen ounces. How was that possible?

Nina is a tall, freckled red-headed woman in her early 30's, who wears her thick wavy hair pulled back in a pony-tail. She has natural beauty that inspires thoughts of faded blue jeans, bare feet and the sunny music of the 70's, like *Ventura Highway* and *Saturday in the Park*. An aura of sadness should have en-gulfed her and the entire room, but there was a tenor of bright, undaunted energy resonating from somewhere deep inside her -- apparently unvexed by the possibility that the tiny new person she is madly in love with may be among the ones who don't make it out of here.

The wires keeping Nina's bright red baby alive looked like a tangle of spaghetti. There was one to deliver oxygen, one to monitor oxygen, one for heart rate, one for intravenous medications, one for delivering liquid food into the veins and one for delivering it through the nose.

"I'm not the most popular person around here," she said, as one of the nurses warned her that her friend, meaning me, would not be able to stay long because there was a medical procedure scheduled.

Another nurse came in immediately and opened the clear plastic lid on the incubator. I could almost feel her cold hands on my own leg as she pulled the sleeping baby's ankle to straighten her leg. She removed an oxygen monitor from her tiny foot and replaced it with another, for what reason, I could not tell. Sophia stretched one hand over her head and straightened the opposite leg stiff until it trembled. There was an icy veneer to the nurse's face, made unnaturally pale by a thick plastering of ivory make-up.

"You're not going to be able to hold her today," the nurse said to Nina without looking at her. "She's desat-ing. This might be a good day to go home and get some rest."

"I'm fine," Nina said.

"You should use days like this to get stuff done," the nurse continued. "Be with the rest of your kids."

"They're fine," Nina said. "We've got lots of help with them at home."

"Suit yourself," she said closing the lid on the incubator and covering it with a specially-made blanket, sewn to fit it. It reminded me of how you would cover a bird cage at night. Nina looked at the cover until the nurse had left the room.

"What have they got against you?" I asked.

"They know I don't trust them," she whispered.

"Why not?"

"The doctors didn't want to treat Sophia," she said, peaking under the cover. "They said she wasn't worth saving -- from a quality of life standpoint."

"Not worth saving?"

"Translation: Costs too much money to keep her alive. Socialized systems don't want to deal with that kind of burden."

"That's terrible. It's all about money."

"Well, it's not just the hospital stay, which can cost upwards of $5,000 or more a day," Nina explained. "Ever since they've gotten good at saving these babies at earlier and earlier gestations, the schools have been flooded with more and more disabilities. Hyperactive kids who have short attention spans, behavioral problems and learning disabilities. They need special ed, they need therapy. Yes, it's a drain on the system. But I don't know how you can put a price tag on a child -- hyperactive or not."

I was stunned by how savvy this woman was for someone who had been thrown into a maternal nightmare less than 10 days ago. I have trouble formulating a coherent question when I take one of my kids to the doctor for a heat rash. I would later learn that Nina is no novice. Sophia is her third preemie. She had four miscarriages before the first one was born and two more between each of the next two. The second of her two live children was born even smaller than Sophia -- at one pound two ounces. Keeping her alive required quite a fight, Nina said.

I just kept thinking of the Agatha Christi quote: "A mother's love for her child is like nothing else in the world. It knows no law, no pity. It dares all things, and crushes down remorselessly all that stands in its path."

Nina handed me her phone, with a family photo displayed. "No one is going to tell me this wasn't worth saving," she said.

She and her tanned, blonde husband are each holding a tiny girl in curly blonde pigtails. Each of the girls is wearing gold-rimmed round glasses and a bashful smile typical of toddlers being photographed. The girls look about 2 and 3 years old, but they are 3 and almost 5. I told Nina how beautiful they were as I handed the phone back. Then, we sat in silence for a few minutes, staring at the orange and blue long-neck dinosaurs printed on the fabric of the incubator's cover.

"Nina, I have to be honest," I said, "because I can tell you can see right through to the heart of things. Father sent me here to pray with you, and I haven't the foggiest idea how to do that."

Nina smiled. "It's just nice of you to come," she said, placing her hand on mine. "You don't have to worry about what or how to pray. The Holy Spirit will guide you. Maybe you're here because you're meant to be the witness of a great miracle."

I smiled at her. "A miracle?"

"If you have any doubt they can happen, stick around."

A different nurse came in, pushing a large machine. This nurse was bone thin with wrists that reminded me of knees on a newborn doe. "We're going to do an MRI now, so I'll need you both to step out. You can come back in about 30 minutes, OK?"

"What's the MRI for?" Nina asked, not budging from her seat.

"Doctor ordered one of the brain. To check for PVL."

"She had one last week."

I stepped out in the hallway and waited for Nina.

"Yes, we need to see if there have been any more brain bleeds since then," the nurse said.

"Can I stay?" Nina asked.

"This is a very tight space," the nurse said. "We need some room, so we ask that all visitors step out. We'll be done in no time."

In the hallway, Nina mumbled, "I am not a visitor. I am a mother."

"Is there a chapel here?" I asked, amazed at the wisdom of my own idea.

We sat silently in dimly-lit peace. I hoped Nina would be soothed by the red, blue and yellow light streaming in through the long, skinny stained glass windows on either side of the chapel. The beams of dusty light met in the center aisle, between the two rows of wooden pews, crossing just under the large plaster dove hung in the center of the back wall. When Nina knelt, so did I. I heard her whispering a Hail Mary under her breath and I joined her. I said half of my Hail Mary's for Nina's child and the other half for mine.

Outside the chapel, Nina thanked me for coming.

"Do you have children, Terry?"

"Yes, three," I said.

"Please, ask them to pray. The prayers of children are powerful."

As I drove home, I felt like I had entered a false world. I felt detached from it as you would from a television program that you've seen a thousand times. The other drivers, pedestrians and diners at sidewalk cafes were like fictional characters, all moving about with inane concerns. "Is that traffic light going to stay green long enough for me to make it? Why didn't I remember to take the chicken out of the freezer? Is my bra strap showing?" Something happens to you when you've just stepped out of a place where there is a membrane-thin line between life and death. Suddenly, the triviality in which most people live their daily lives becomes unsettling -- maybe even repulsive. You no longer care to live in this oblivious and incidental place. I fought the urge to make a U-turn and drive back to the NICU. I knew I would not be welcomed back by the nurses, though, and I didn't want to risk adding to the animosity they already feel toward Nina. I would wait until tomorrow.

I was anxious to tell the girls what I had seen today, but when I got home, Katie had engaged her siblings and Lily in another round of her trademark "would you rather?" form of interrogations, while everyone stood around the kitchen island eating crunchy foods out of crackly bags.

"Would you rather be in a tornado or a hurricane?" Katie asked.

"A hurricane," Laura replied.

"Would you rather be in a tornado or be struck by lightning?"

"Tornado," Laura said.

"Me too," said Katie.

"Would you rather be in a fire or a tornado?"

Laura chose a tornado again. "Anything but a fire," she added.

"If you were in a fire in a high rise building, would you jump or burn?" Katie asked.

"Jump."

"What about you, Beth?" said Katie.

"I'm not playing this game," Beth snapped.

"Just choose," Katie insisted.

"Jump," she said through the clenched stickiness of cheese puff-covered molars.

"Good choice," Laura confirmed. "I heard burning to death and drowning are the two worse ways to die."

Oh no. As if Katie needed any more ideas. "Would you rather drown or die in a fire?" she asked.

"Neither," Laura said. "I just said they were both horrible."

"Just choose," Katie nagged.

"OK. Drown."

"What about you Beth?" Katie asked.

"Not playing," she clarified, apathetically.

"Just choose," Katie begged. "Please?"

"I would rather jump out of a towering inferno into an F-5 tornado, get whipped around until my head nearly pops off, then have the violent winds body slam me into shark-infested waters, have my flesh torn off and drown -- than be in this conversation with you."

"That's sick," Katie said. And thus ended another morbid line of questioning.

Very strange that Beth made reference to shark-infested waters. It was like an echo with a five-hour delay.

"All of humanity is on a ship, moving through shark infested waters in a great and terrible storm," Father Fitz had told me. "Some people are teetering over the edge, taunting the sharks with the blood dripping from their wounds. Some have climbed up the bird's nest pole, in a hysteria so frenzied, they are bound to fall to their death before the ship even has time to sink. Some are standing back watching with disinterest, believing that the belief in storms is just plain old silly and that the lightning and the thunder and the wind and the rain must have been created with some sort of special effects. And as for the sharks, they have to be mechanical like *Jaws'* Bruce. Some people are standing out on deck, waiting to watch the feeding frenzy when someone falls in. Some are below deck sleeping, unaware that they are even on a boat. And then, there are a few wearing life vests and shark repellent. But we're all on this ship together. All of humanity boarded the ship, headed for a common destiny. Some will make it. Some won't. I've decided my life means nothing if I don't help as many fellow travelers as I can to survive."

"And how do you survive?" I asked Father.

"A life vest," he said, picking up the crucifix he wears around his neck. "And-" He pulled a wooden rosary out of his pocket and dangled it between him and me. "Shark repellent."

8

COMFORT CARE

This morning, I awoke thinking about Auntie Bev. I thought of how hard it must have been for her to go through the motions day after day, taking care of us, when she felt nothing.

I had always thought she was highly intelligent because she read so much. Then, as I got older, I began to realize she was reading not for an education, but for an escape. She was not fond of the life that had been laid out for her. Her books provided an alternate reality for a given part of her day. Meanwhile, those of us who were not between the covers of a book were exiled to a cold and often lonely landscape. I never really got over my mother's death. She was everything I longed for, and Auntie Bev provided nothing of her, even though the same blood ran through their veins.

I try very hard to make my children feel loved, even if I don't feel it. But I sometimes wonder if I'm successful. I wonder if Beth somehow sensed my lack of emotional attachment to my family and retreated into her own shell. I know that my own tee-nage rebellion began with a realization that Auntie Bev did not deserve the respect I had once thought she did. There were many reasons for this. But the most prominent was the way she treated Lily. I began to hypothesize that she treated her different from me and Jimmy, not because she was younger, but because she didn't like her as much. It wasn't that she allowed us more privileges that bothered me. That would have been logical since we were older and able-minded. It was the little things, like serving her last and giving her whatever anyone else didn't want. It was the opposite of what you would normally do for the baby of the family. I always felt sorry for Lily because she never got anything chocolate. Her saliva would flow faster than she could swallow it and she would drool it out all over her face and clothing. So Auntie Bev always gave her vanilla ice cream instead. I felt bad for Lily because I knew she was missing the best flavor in life. One day, after Auntie Bev had given us our ice cream cones, she went off into her room to read. I traded my chocolate cone for Lily's vanilla. Lily smiled wide and said "tae," which meant "thank you." I've never seen anyone take so long to eat an ice cream cone, and I was nervous that Auntie Bev would come back out to the kitchen before Lily had finished. I kept the basket of napkins under my hand and just kept wiping the chocolate drool, so it wouldn't end up on Lily's clothes or on the gold damask table cloth. Jimmy served as look-out, facing the hallway so he could warn me if Auntie Bev was coming and we could quickly switch the cones back again. The next time, it was Jimmy who offered to trade with Lily. From then on, we took turns giving up our chocolate ice cream any time it was prudent and we could safely pull it off. We never did get caught.

Somehow emboldened by the memory of the courage we had as children, I drew strength from a place deep within and marched into Jake's office. Wearing, not a silky black night gown, but a baggy pair of fleece Bermuda shorts and an old T-shirt, I made my request.

"Jake, I really want you to have a vasectomy reversal."

"A what?"

"A reversal. So we can try for another baby."

"You want me to get unfixed?"

"Yes. Well, actually, I want you to get fixed. I want us to fix what we broke."

"Why? It was your idea to get me snipped in the first place."

That was back when I wanted to shorten my forever with you, I thought, but how do I tell you that? "I know, Darling," I said, "but I've changed my mind."

"So, I have to put my jewels under the knife every time you change your mind?" His voice was slightly raised. "That's ludicrous."

His words rang true. It was ludicrous. How do you convince your husband that he should be happy about all of this because, while you once were plotting your escape from him, now you are resigned to spend the rest of your life with him.

I can tell you the exact moment when I gave up hope of ever finding a justification for leaving, for starting my life over and possibly finding someone who might be interested in searching the depths of my dormant soul for a flicker of passion. I can tell you the exact moment I realized it was not going to happen. Not as I watched my hulkish husband haul 113 boxes and eight rooms of furniture into a moving van. Not as I witnessed his dawn-to-dusk driving halfway across the country with three incessantly chatty females and a fourth who refused to acknowledge his existence. Not as I heard him tell the realtor our new home must be on the public transit route and in close proximity to the zoo for the sake of his sister's-in-law budding art career. Not as I watched him rebuild his own career, stone by stone, in new and unknown territory. No, these were not the moments that held my future captive, although any one of them ought to have been. But the thing of which I speak was something I witnessed through a window when a volleyball hit the pane and directed my attention to a very large, handsome, muscular, somewhat obtuse and reticent man, who picked a 37-year-old sobbing woman with Down Syndrome out of the mud, wiped the hair out of her eyes with his knuckle, planted his forehead on hers and made a brief statement that changed her tears instantly into laughter. In that moment I realized the man I married was far too decent to give me the justification I wanted. He has gone beyond the duty of family man into the realm of paragon. So now the question isn't whether I will ever be in the position to feel deep love again. The question is, given an average human lifespan, how will I get through the next 12,000 days without it?

"What brought all this on, Terry?" Jake's voice was softer now as I stared out his office window.

"Well, initially, Lily. She really wants a baby and I know she'll never have one of her own.""

"Oh, Babe," Jake said. "You don't know what you're asking."

"I do, Honey, I do know," I pleaded. "I know it's huge, but I'm begging you."

"She already has a puppy, Babe. Can't that be enough?"

"Honey," I admonished. "You know that's not the same."

"Can't you just rent a baby? Start a day care or something?"

"I want to be pregnant, Jake. I want Lily to come to the ultrasound appointments with me -- and cut the umbilical cord. With your help of course."

"Of course."

"Jake, she'll never have this experience in her life. And it's such an incredible experience. You remember, don't you?"

"Sure, I do. They gave me a vasectomy, not a lobotomy."

"Well, they do say men think with their --"

"Honey, come on."

"Who knows?" I said smiling. "Maybe you'll have a son."

"I don't need a son," he said. "Every female in this house is a sports freak."

"You are greatly outnumbered here, Jake, and you know it."

"Yes, and there's a 50-50 chance I'll be more outnumbered after another baby." He sighed and ran his hand down the length of my arm. "Oh, Terry, I thought we decided we didn't want any more."

"That's when times were tougher, Jake."

"And they're not tough now -- with all the issues with Beth and Lily to take care of? And another teen and a tween and a kleptomaniac dog who doesn't remember who we are and barks at us whenever we come back down the stairs?"

"The girls would be a tremendous help," I countered. "You know how much they love babies."

"Oh, Terry."

"Why shouldn't we have a baby, Jake?" I said. "We love each other. We've got no marital problems, no financial difficulties. So why shouldn't we?"

"Because we're old?"

"Is that what you think?" I climbed onto his lap, straddling him in his office chair, and gave him a deep, long kiss. I felt his tension melt away.

"And how much does it cost?" he said, coming up for air.

"Like, in the thousands." My forehead was pressed against his.

"How many thousands?"

"Ten."

"Good grief, Terry." The tension returned, as he pushed me slightly and my head moved away from his.

"OK, Jake. Just don't answer right now. Just think about it for a while."

He said nothing.

"OK? Will you promise to think about it?" I prodded.

"OK, Babe," he resigned. "I promise." He pulled me to him. His firm chest pressed into my breasts. "Now show me again how *not* old we are." The office chair squeaked in mournful rhythm with our desires.

****

I returned to the NICU today. I was surprised to see the ventilator gone and Sophia's tiny body lying in a small open crib, peacefully swaddled in a flannel blanket imprinted with yellow ducks and blue bubbles. My heart leapt at the sight of the miracle that had overtaken her. Sometime in the last five days, she had somehow managed to shed attachments to the equipment that had been necessary to keep her alive, except for a single IV. Nina had her back to the door, sitting in a rocking chair next to the crib, rubbing Sophia's tiny hand between her index finger and thumb. I touched Nina on the shoulder, my face bursting with a smile. As she turned, my heart crashed. Her face was tense with worry, her eyes reddened by an inexhaustible flow of tears and encircled by purple rings of sleep deprivation.

"Nina," I said. "What's wrong? What's happening?"

"They've decided to discontinue treatment," she said.

"Why?" My voice came out as a gasp.

"Her brain scans were not good," Nina said, in a matter-of-fact tone. "In cases of such severe PVL, it's not humane to artificially prolong a life, so they say. Basically, they don't want to waste their resources."

I sat down in the rocking chair next to Nina. "There's nothing anyone can do? A lawyer? A judge?" I asked. I couldn't believe the story of this life was going to end this way. I had fully expected a miracle, even though I've never been sure that I believe in them. Nina had assured me there would be one and she's the type of person who isn't wrong about such matters.

"No," she said. "The feds decide. Not the patients. Not the parents. The bureaucrats. We have arrived at a scary place."

I noticed now that Sophia's face was frighteningly pale and the skin around her lips had a bluish tint. She startled in her sleep as I stared at her, and her fingers straightened stiff, splayed out into open air like a five-point star. Her fingernails were blue. I wanted to know if there was any chance that she could survive without medical treatment, but how do you ask a mother that question? I assumed Nina was operating under the assumption that there was a chance. Every mother would have to -- or else find herself in a heap of sobbing grief on the floor.

"When did they unplug everything?" I asked.

"Yesterday," Nina said. "We've just been holding her as much as we can. Her heart rate falls dangerously low and her oxygen levels drop because she forgets to breathe. I know it sounds terrible, but I just pinch her ear or thump her foot or her diaper until she remembers. And the nurses, they just look at me as if I'm abusing her. I know they're thinking I should just let her go -- peacefully."

Her face contorted with sadness. "They say she will likely die within 48 hours."

"I'm so sorry, Nina," I said. I felt a lump suddenly form in my throat as I realized I had let this woman down. She had asked me to have my children pray. What if that could have made a difference?

Nina wiped her face with the flat, open insides of her hands. "Well, we don't know what's going to happen," she said, sniffing back tears. "We do, however, know that they are not God. And they will not decide, even though they operate under illusions that they do. Much to their dismay, this child just may live. She may be a burden to society, she may be a pain in the neck to her teachers. But she darned well may live." She reached into the crib and picked Sophia up, holding the baby close to her chest and breaking down into a full sob.

"She's so beautiful," I said.

She handed Sophia to me and leaned back in her chair, placing her hands on her head and gasping for air. I was surprised at how little Sophia weighed. I stared into the baby's face. Her helplessness caused a profound aching in my chest. I closed my eyes and rocked her. I felt just as helpless.

"Hail Mary full of grace, the Lord is with thee. Blessed art thou among women and blessed is the fruit of thy womb, Jesus."

Nina joined in. "Holy Mary, Mother of God, pray for us sinners, now and at the hour of our death. Amen."

In the hallway, on the way out, I ran into Nina's husband, carrying two large drinks from downstairs. I recognized him from the family photo. I introduced myself as a friend of Father Fitz's. He told me his wife was having a difficult time accepting it, but there was no hope for his baby daughter and the only medical treatment she would receive from here on out is what the hospital calls "comfort care." Everyone was just waiting for Sophia to die. Everyone except Nina, who was waiting for a miracle.

9

THE SWORD

I never undecorate a Christmas tree without thinking about the Christmas when Lily was six. She had misplaced her glasses about a week before Christmas. All of us children were offered grand rewards if we could help them to materialize. We hunted and we searched. Under beds, behind dressers, inside cabinets and drawers. In the course of the two weeks, Auntie Bev took everything out of all the closets in the house and placed everything back in, neat and organized, but still no glasses. Auntie Bev decided we would just have to consider them gone forever and order another pair.

"I know as soon as we fork out $250 for new ones, we're going to find them," she foreboded. It was uncanny how well Auntie Bev could predict gloom. The good stuff, not so much.

Well, on Dec. 23, Auntie Bev ordered Lily new glasses, fully resigned to the fate of finding them the day after she picked up the new pair. The optician said it would take a week to ten days for the glasses to come in.

On January 2, we set about taking the ornaments off the tree. Auntie Bev asked us all to help to get it done quickly because she found taking decorations down so depressing.

"Uh, Auntie Bev," I said, talking to her through the tree. "Are you still offering a reward to whoever finds Lily's glasses?"

"No," she said, dryly. "Now that I've ordered another pair, who ever finds them is getting a spanking."

"Uh-oh," I said. I played along with what I knew was a joke for two reasons. First, that's the kind of sense of humor Auntie Bev had and I had become well accustomed to it. Second, she was not a spanker.

"Why?" She peaked around the tree at me. I dangled Lily's glasses between my finger and thumb and gave her a sheepish grin.

"Where did you find those?" she asked.

"Right here on this branch," I said. "I guess Lily wanted to decorate the tree with them."

"Fabulous," she said sarcastically. Then she shrugged, as she resumed rolling the garland. "Well, at least she'll have a second pair in case she wants to hide them for the Easter egg hunt."

I continued to take the gold sequined balls and the white ones that looked like snowballs off the tree. It was my routine to get those first, then move onto the one-of-a-kind ornaments that have names and dates on the bottom. Every year, Uncle Jack would take us to Wal-Mart and let us choose one new ornament. He did this even after he and Auntie Bev split up. We'd bring our new ornaments home and mark the date on them with Sharpie so we would have a collection to take with us when we moved out on our own someday. My favorite was -- and still is -- the one marked 2017, which is a Santa taking a well-deserved break to warm his butt by the fireplace.

"Speaking of second pairs," said Auntie Bev. "I wonder why the new ones haven't come in. Probably the holidays slowing them down. I'll call tomorrow."

The call proved, once again, that God must have been in our corner. The woman at the eyeglass place apologized profusely. Somehow the order had been lost in cyberspace and the lab hadn't even begun working on the glasses yet. Auntie Bev was able to cancel the order without being charged a dime. Lily jumped up and down and yelled "Yay!" when I gave her glasses back. Apparently she had forgotten that she had used them to contribute to the yuletide cheer. The gold frames really would have added a festive touch to the tree, had Lily chosen a showier spot.

****

My group didn't meet during the month of December because of the busyness of Christmas, so I didn't see Father Fitz, which is where I would have been likely to get an update on Sophia. I'm sure he didn't cut out on Nina like I did.

I never did return to the NICU. It's not that I didn't care what happened to Sophia. But I knew what the final answer was going to be for her, and I didn't know how to thrust myself into the midst of a grieving family. I decided two visits would not render me important enough in Nina's life to be missed. But I often have fantasies of running into Nina in the grocery store or in the park. She is flanked by her two little blonde girls and is carrying a third in her arms -- all pink and plump with blonde curls. I think about what Nina said to me -- that maybe I was sent to Sophia's bedside to witness a miracle. If that is the case, I failed myself. Father had sent me there to do something radical. And I don't think running away qualifies. On the other hand, maybe I was just there to pray. Maybe that, in itself, *is* the miracle.

At the first meeting of the new year, we explored the suffering of women.

"When a woman is in travail she has sorrow, because her hour has come; but when she is delivered of the child, she no longer remembers the anguish, for joy that a child is born into the world."

This is the reason, it is said, that women have more than one child. I never realized before reading John Paul II's encyclical that the amnesia of childbirth has a Biblical basis.

"The first part of Christ's words refers to the pangs of childbirth ... at the same time these words indicate the link that exists between the woman's motherhood and the Paschal Mys-

tery. For this mystery also includes the Mother's sorrow at the foot of the Cross - the Mother who through faith shares in the amazing mystery of her Son's "self-emptying" ... As we contemplate this Mother, whose heart "a sword has pierced," our thoughts go to all the suffering women in the world, suffering either physically or morally ... It is difficult to enumerate these sufferings; it is difficult to call them all by name. We may recall her maternal care for her children, especially when they fall sick or fall into bad ways; the death of those most dear to her; the loneliness of mothers forgotten by their grown up children; the loneliness of widows; the sufferings of women who struggle alone to make a living; and women who have been wronged or exploited. Then there are the sufferings of consciences as a result of sin, which has wounded the woman's human or maternal dignity: the wounds of consciences which do not heal easily. With these sufferings too we must place ourselves at the foot of the Cross.

"But the words of the Gospel about the woman who suffers when the time comes for her to give birth to her child, immediately afterwards express joy: it is "the joy that a child is born into the world". This joy too is referred to the Paschal Mystery, to the joy which is communicated to the Apostles on the day of Christ's Resurrection: "So you have sorrow now" (these words were said the day before the Passion); "but I will see you again and your hearts will rejoice, and no one will take your joy from you."

Late in the afternoon, I e-mailed Jake the link to the website I'd found with the rodeo cowboy. This is the type of sales pitch that would appeal to Jake. He has always been a man's man. There is no wimpishness about him whatsoever, and if he hadn't become a computer programmer he could have very well been a cowboy or a lumberjack -- if there were any cows or trees left. He would have liked a steady supply of dirt for his fingernails.

I wish Jake could understand about this baby. Sometimes I'll be sitting, reading a magazine or combing my hair, and I'll just feel like I have to take inventory -- like someone is missing.

Who have I forgotten to worry about? Jake's meeting with a client. Katie's in her room reading. Laura is at a sleep-over. Beth is listening to morbid music in her room. Lily is working a late shift. Yes, they're all accounted for. Or are they? Isn't there someone else?

****

"Mom, I think I have bumps on my rear," hollered Katie from the bathroom. "It hurts and it's itchy. Let me look in the mirror."

A short pause.

"No," she decided "I don't see anything."

I longed for the days when I had few enough inhibitions to talk about my butt. And the bumps that may or may not be on it. Round about the time we start to hold our stomachs in, we cease to talk about our butts. We neglect them, as if they were not a part of us or we could make them go away by not mentioning them. There's only two ways you can be unvexed by such imperfections as dimply butts and belly flab. You can be a child or you can be Lily.

Lily will slap herself in the belly to see the fat quiver. The sight of it makes her giggle, which makes it jiggle all the more. A belly, to her, presents no occasion for shame. It is great entertainment. I know she would have had a blast being pregnant.

Today, after loading my groceries in the car, a woman struck up a conversation with me. We were both struggling to get our shopping carts to fall in line with the rest of the ones collecting in the parking lot. She was a woman in her mid-30s with a beach-ball belly.

"These stubborn things," she said, yanking her cart into position behind another.

"They have minds of their own, don't they," I agreed.

As we were both walking back to our cars, she looked down over her black tank top. "Look at me," she said, brushing her shirt off. "I've always got stuff all over me. I'm like a kid."

"Just wait until that one comes out," I said motioning to her belly. I was remembering how when Beth was little, my shirt was never dry. She had such horrible reflux, she would drench me in spit-up after every feeding. The strange thing was, I came to associate the smell with my new baby and I actually grew to like it. I would stand in the laundry room taking long sniffs of her burp cloths before putting them in the washer.

"Oh, I can wait," the pregnant woman said. "This will be my fourth. I've always got boogers all over me." She continued disgustedly brushing at invisible debris. I felt sorry for her children. This is not the way mothers should feel about their children's boogers. I wanted to tell this woman that boogers should be worn with pride, like Girl Scout badges. Or purple hearts. Or a general's stars. This is how I see my emerging wrinkles and my seven gray hairs. I refuse to cover them up. I have earned these, through tears and toil, and the whole world is going to stand witness to my war wounds.

"Believe it or not, you'll miss those boogers some day," I told that woman. "I'd give anything to have a fourth in my belly."

"People who are not pregnant always love pregnancy," she said, hoisting herself up into her SUV. "Have a great day."

It was a nice sentiment from a sarcastic, hormonal pregnant lady, but my day hadn't been great, and it was about to get worse.

I hadn't even gotten all the groceries unloaded from my car into the house when the clamor found me. "Mom, Mom, Mom," Laura was screaming like a siren -- the tone reserved for reacting to serious affronts by siblings. The obnoxious sound was getting closer. I could tell by the Doppler effect. "Someone stole my money. Someone stole my $100 I got for my birthday."

"Hang on, Laura," I said, setting a bag down on the counter. "Maybe you just misplaced it. Let's not jump to conclusions. There've been no cat burglaries in this neighborhood lately."

"But I put it in my top dresser drawer and now it's gone," she said. "Like you always say, Mom, things don't just grow legs and walk away." Your own words always sound so ridiculous coming from someone else's mouth.

"Maybe you put it somewhere else and you thought you put it in your dresser," I said. "Did you look around?"

"It's always been in my drawer," she said. "I see it every morning when I get my underwear. I saw it last night after I came home from swimming. But now it's gone."

Katie took the opportunity to inject some intrigue as children who are zealous readers often do. She walked to the windows and made a drama of checking the locks. "No sign of entry here," she said. She swung around and squinted dramatically.

"Maybe the thief is among us."

"That's exactly what I was thinking," Laura said.

Katie looked a little surprised that her theory was being considered. Laura fixed a blank stare on her. "Well, don't look at me," said Katie. "I'm not a common criminal."

"No," Laura said in agreement. "You're not evil enough to steal from your own sister. But I know someone who is." She ran up the stairs, and I knew I had better follow. Nothing good could come of this.

Laura flung Beth's door open hard enough to bounce it off the doorstop.

"Where's my money, Beth," she demanded.

Beth yanked the ear phones out and looked at her with a mixture of confusion and boredom. "What money?" Every emotion Beth displayed in the past two years has been mixed with boredom.

"You know what money," Laura stood her ground.

"I don't know what you're talking about."

"My birthday money. The $100 bill Dad gave me."

"I have no idea where it is," Beth said.

"No one else would have taken it, Beth," Laura said.

"Look, I promised you I wouldn't steal from you again, Laura, and I haven't, so just leave me alone." She started to replace the ear phones, but Beth grabbed them away from her.

"Hey, what's your problem?" Beth yelled. "Give those back."

Katie and I watched from the doorway. I figured I would let them go as long as no one was drawing blood.

"Give me my money back," Laura yelled. She was typically not a screamer, but her sense of right and wrong had been offended. And her buying power had been severely affected.

"For the last time, sister dear, I did not take your money." Beth grabbed the earphones back and proceeded to stuff them into her ears. "Now, thank you for seeing yourself out."

"Why am I supposed to believe you, Beth?"

"Because I told you I wouldn't do it again."

"And I'm supposed to believe that you're just a thief, not a liar, right?"

No answer. Beth had a way of tuning everything out that was not beneficial to her state of mind. She closed her eyes and resumed her tunes.

Laura stormed out, past me and Katie, without looking at us, stomped to her room and slammed her door.

"Beth stole from Laura?" Katie asked. Now Katie is far from obtuse, but she couldn't quite grasp this possibility. People her age are still surprised by corruption, especially among blood relatives.

Through Laura's closed door, I heard drawers opening and shutting in a frenzied, fruitless search. I knocked on her door and told her I'd replace the money. I felt bad that she was out of the money she had been saving to buy a laptop. But I felt worse that I had raised someone who could be legitimately blamed for its disappearance. I had my doubts that Beth had kept her promise. And I was scared to death of what $100 could buy.

Later, after everyone was asleep, I snuck into Beth's room and took her purse down to the family room. I dumped its contents onto the ottoman: an MP3 player, cell phone, tampon, hair clip, gum wrapper. I opened the zipper portion of the purse and found three dollar bills and some change and a pack of Newport cigarettes. I was relieved not to find the $100. I was curious to see how many cigarettes she had left. I opened the pack. There were two. One was wrapped in a $100 bill.

****

In the morning, I gave the money back to Laura. She felt bad that I had to spend another $100 on her birthday, but I told her it was not a big deal. She promised if she ever found the original hundred, she would give it back to me, but she very much doubted that she ever would. Beth hasn't mentioned anything about the disappearance of the money or her cigarettes. I know that she knows that I am a snoop, and she knows that I know she is a thief. That is the unspoken secret Beth and I will keep between us. And I am quite certain neither one of us feels a bit of shame.

10

EGGS

I suppose I shouldn't be surprised that I got my period again. For years, we have forced God's hand away. He may have had a gift for us, or maybe several, and we refused to reach out our hands and accept them. Although the surgeon was practically giddy about his work on Jake's vas deferens, it would be ridiculous for us to think we could snap our fingers and order up another kid. But that still doesn't stop the aching I have inside. It's a strange kind of grief when you've lost something that you've never had.

Sometimes I get a craving for something, but I don't know what it is. I park myself inside the pantry, surveying the shelves. I stand with the refrigerator door hanging open, peering in. Nothing I see makes me want to eat it. I think about getting in the car and driving to a fast-food place or the grocery store to pick something up. But nothing I can think of makes me happy. So, it occurs to me maybe whatever I'm craving hasn't been invented yet. Recall that there was a time in history when ice cream did not exist. The people who lived back then in that dark, horrible time must have had cravings for it. But they didn't know what they were craving. This is how it is for me and my baby. I don't know who I'm missing, but I miss.

Infertility is an empty pain, one without tears to cleanse a wound. One without even a wound really. A woundless pain is difficult, if not impossible, to treat. At least when you're bleeding, you can use a tourniquet. You might lose a limb, but you save your life. But depression gives you nothing to target with any kind of accuracy. Even if there were a remedy, where would you apply it? Depression encompasses a larger space than your body. It is in your soul, which extends past the parameters of your skin.

Where do I find sympathy? Not from childless couples, who would view me fortunate to have three children. Not from countless fertile couples, who would be glad to trade in their fertility for a worry-free love life. And certainly not from your best friend who talked you into having your husband "fixed" -- as if the ability to give life to another human being means he is broken. I know I've been saying we're trying to do this whole baby thing for Lily, but if I told the entire truth, I'd admit there's more to it than that.

Frannie would think I'm crazy for what I did. The last time I talked to her, several months ago, I stepped around the issue. I asked her if she ever regretted Brad's vasectomy.

"Oh, my goodness, no," she said. "I could never do the whole baby thing all over again. Don't get me wrong. I enjoyed every minute of it when my kids were little, but it was exhausting. I think people forget how exhausting it is."

"But don't you remember how crazy in love you are with that tiny little person?"

"Yeah, but it's so nice now that the kids are older. It's nice to have a little freedom back. Besides, you wouldn't want to be fertile right now. At our age, you're dealing with the whole high-risk pregnancy thing. I'm not sure how fair that would be to the baby. Maybe the fact that people lose their fertility as they get older, maybe that's just nature's way of working things out. You never know, maybe even without the vasectomy, you wouldn't get pregnant. There are lots of women who wait too long. But you have your three beautiful children, which you had at the perfect time in your life. Now it's time for a new chapter."

"You mean a high risk for Down Syndrome?" I said.

"Well, not just that." I suspected Frannie had spoken before thinking, that she had momentarily forgotten she was talking to someone whose life was eternally intertwined with one of those "high risk" people.

Although Jake and I have procreated three children, now that I know exactly what is involved, the chances of anyone ever giving birth seem rather ridiculous. An ovary has to ovulate. The egg has to be good. A fallopian tube has to pick up the egg. The cervical mucus must be hospitable to the sperm and free of any antibodies. The sperm has to reach the fallopian tube. The sperm has to blindly and by chance find the egg. It has to knock away at the shell until it penetrates the egg. One and only one must fertilize the egg. The embryo has to survive the trip from the fallopian tube to the uterus. The endometrial cavity has to be receptive to the incoming embryo. The embryo must find a welcoming lining and attach to the uterus. The woman's hormonal environment must be adequate for the embryo's development. Her uterus must be structurally sound. The placenta must stay intact. And viola, nine months later, a baby.

If I spend too much time thinking about it, the whole concept of conception seems unreal. It was two weeks before my 11th birthday when my friend Stephanie told me exactly how babies are made. At first, I didn't believe her. It all sounded so farfetched. Auntie Bev had told me babies are made when a man and woman lie down naked together. The rest of it, I wouldn't have guessed. But it explained a lot.

The way I had it in my head was that when a man and woman want to have a baby, they take off their clothes and lie down and some kind of magic makes the baby start to form in the woman's belly. So, if they don't want a baby, they don't lie down naked. So, why would Mom plan to have a baby by lying down with that man she was never going to see again? With Stephanie's new information, I was able to see the full picture. Mom wasn't trying to make a baby with that man. She was just trying to have some fun. But a baby they did make. I began to see Lily as a mistake instead of a choice -- an unfortunate consequence of doing something bad. This is the subconscious foundation on which was built a nagging question, which much to my horror, one day escaped my lips.

I had spent quite a number of hours on my science fair project, demonstrating how a change in air pressure created by a lit match would force a hard-boiled egg into a bottle. I chose this experiment because it provided an excuse to light a match, which Auntie Bev had finally let me do.

On the day my project was due, Lily found the egg in a Ziploc bag next an empty iced-tea bottle on the kitchen counter, decided it was breakfast and ate it eight minutes before the school bus was due to arrive. There was no way I could cook a ten-minute egg in eight minutes. In a flash, all the ruined assignments of the six years of my school career came rushing through my brain, projecting themselves like videos on the inside of my skull. The scribbled-on math papers, the vandalized composition, the dismembered caveman diorama. The projector in my skull turned the screen to bright red.

"Why did you ever have to be born?" I screamed at Lily as I burst into tears.

She looked at me stunned, her eyes wide and frightened. Tiny bits of egg debris framed her mouth, which had been shocked open by my cruel question. I ran to my room and slammed the door, resigned to an unexcused absence, an F on my science project and an irreparably broken relationship with my only sister. Auntie Bev heard the slam as she was coming out of the shower. She shot down the hall wrapped in her towel, water droplets still puddling on her shoulders. She flung open the door and demanded to know what the matter was. I became even angrier then with Lily. It was her fault that I couldn't even properly hole myself up in my room. All of the locks in our house had been disabled because Lily had locked herself in one too many times.

"What's the matter?" Auntie Bev asked again, this time softer, upon seeing the volume of tears.

"Lily ate my science project," I said.

"The egg?"

"Yes," I blubbered.

"Figures," Auntie Bev said. She let out a heavy sigh. "Well, get your stuff together, Honey. The bus is going to be here any minute."

"But the science fair is today," I whined.

"I know, I know," Auntie Bev said. "I'll bring an egg by later."

We rushed into the kitchen. Auntie Bev helped me gather my things and shuffled me toward the door. Jimmy had spent the weekend with Jack on a camping trip and Jack was to take him straight to school that morning. So just Lily and I were to board the bus.

"Where's Lily?" Auntie Bev asked.

"I don't know," I said wiping my nose on my sleeve. "She's probably hiding."

It's what she did when someone was mad at her.

"You check her room," Auntie Bev said. "I'll watch for the bus."

She wasn't in her room or in the bathroom or in Auntie Bev's room.

The bus pulled up. Auntie Bev told the driver she would be taking us to school and sent him on his way.

We searched behind curtains, in closets, under beds and behind couches. Lily was not in the house. We searched the back yard, and she wasn't there either. We did it all one more time. Still no Lily. We hollered her name into the air all through the house, cajoling, bribing, threatening. Still no Lily. We promised pizza. Still no Lily. This is when we knew for certain she was simply not there.

"Oh, no," Auntie Bev finally said, with a look of horror. "I don't think I had to unlock the top lock to talk to the bus driver. I don't think it was latched."

"She wouldn't have left by herself," I said. "She's never done that before."

Auntie Bev ran for her car keys. "There's a first time for everything," she said. "You stay here in case she comes home. I'm going to look for her."

I felt sick and abandoned as I imagined Lily walking farther and farther from home. I pictured some horrible kidnapper be-friending her and convincing her to come home with him to get French fries and butter bread. We might never see her again. And it was all because of my awful words. Why did I wish her out of existence? How could I be such a monster? She was just hungry. She was just doing what people do when they are hun-gry and they see an egg. I sat in the middle of the kitchen floor, rocking and crying on my knees and praying that God would not punish me by granting the wish that I had uttered out of thought-less anger.

It must have been about fifteen minutes later that I heard the garage door open. I prayed as I ran to the car that I would see Lily in the back seat. And there she was. I jumped into the car and threw my arms around her. She wasn't wearing any shoes.

"Oh, Lily," I sobbed. "Please don't ever do this again."

She smiled and hugged me back.

"I'm sorry I got mad at you, Lily," I said. "Please don't ever go out by yourself again. OK?" I wiped the hair out of her eyes and she wiped mine off my cheek, which had become sticky with tears.

"OK?" I said.

"Yeah," she said.

"Where was she?" I asked Auntie Bev.

"A woman found her and called the police. She said she was just about ready to cross the highway."

"The police?"

"Yeah," she said. "They were talking to Lily when I pulled up. They were trying to figure out where she belonged."

"Was she crying?"

"No, she just had her head down, you know, in her typical shy way."

Within three days, Auntie Bev had installed alarms on all the doors. She told me not to tell anyone about Lily's escape because it was too painful for her to re-tell. The thought of what might have happened if that woman had not stopped her was too much to bear. It was too much for me, too, so I was more than glad never to talk about it again. I never told Auntie Bev what I had said to Lily that morning. I don't think Lily could have understood exactly what it meant, but she knew it was cruel. I was certain that Lily had left the house in tears and had walked off her sorrow by the time Auntie Bev found her. Yes, I was happy to push the whole incident out of my mind. And so, it became the only episode forever lost to our vault of Lily stories.

From then on, I made sure all my science projects were inedible. Or at the very least, that they utilized only green food, which Lily never touched. And I never again wondered why Lily was born. The thought of a world without her was answer enough.

****

Last night, in my dreams, an elderly lady wearing a white crocheted shawl stood at the end of a long hallway. She was holding something in her arms, but she was so far away, I could not make out what it was. She plodded toward me, making slow, but even progress, concentrating very hard on not falling. It seemed like minutes passed and she was still walking. I don't know why I didn't walk toward her, to make her journey shorter. But I stood, as if paralyzed, waiting. Finally she got near enough for me to see that she was carrying a newborn baby, swaddled in a green and blue tartan blanket. I couldn't see the baby's face, so tightly was she pressing the bundle to her chest. I studied the woman's doughy face. She looked vaguely familiar. She extended the baby to me and said "Here's your boy." As I reached out to take him, I was awakened by my alarm clock. I felt deeply cheated. I so wanted to hold that baby and inwardly mourned for him throughout the day. I wondered why my alarm had to go off and ruin my chances of holding him. Late in the afternoon, I came to the conclusion that the alarm belonged to my biological clock and God was trying to tell me my time had run out. At 4:40, I picked up the phone and called the foster care agency. Lily and I are going to have a baby to love, unreceptive eggs and uncooperative sperm notwithstanding.

11

AWE

Tasha is an almost 3-year-old, tiny thing with blue, bewildered eyes and red hair that is contemplating whether it should curl or not. Her arms are delicate and straight, like sticks wrapped in soft, pink skin. They lack the padding necessary to provide any assurance that this child could survive a skipped meal. Her face is blank and unreadable, like the haunting stare of a Botox patient.

Lily scooped Tasha up in her arms and stared into her round eyes, silently begging to save her from any more hardship. Tasha put all her weight into her upper body and thrust it toward the floor. Lily set her down and Tasha went back on her heels and then forward onto her toes and then settled in on flat feet. Lily picked her up again.

Laura stood by Lily, smiling, and picked up Tasha's hand. "Hi sweet girl," she said.

"Can I hold her?" Katie asked, her hands in the shape of a prayer.

Beth just stared at Tasha through half-closed eyes, lids laden with black eye-liner, chin thrust forward. It is the same way she looks at everything from her favorite meal to a dead roach.

"I gonna take care of you," Lily told Tasha, straight into her face.

Tasha made another lunge for the floor, but Lily took no offense. She just giggled and put her down. It's not that Lily

115

doesn't understand the concept of strangers. It's just that, with Lily, the evolution from stranger to loved one is acutely abbreviated. Like time-lapse photography, all the frames are there, moving along in rapid succession, undetectable to the unaided eye. It's the same thing that happened when Lily met Pablo Perez. Heck, I think my attachment mechanism was in time-lapse mode too. Something about the man, but I felt a bit jealous of Lily. I wished Pablo Perez was my father too.

"Do you want to come to our house and play," I asked squatting down to look Tasha in the eye.

"You get to sleep in my room," Katie said, bending over my shoulder to get to Tasha's face.

Tasha pushed her eyebrows together, making her first response of the day.

"She's a cutie," Jake said. He was standing back with Beth, his arms folded across his chest, his rear propped on the table, his feet crossed.

"Does she talk?" Katie asked me, still looking at Tasha.

"She's probably just a little shy right now, Honey," I told her. "And overwhelmed. We're all strangers to her."

"Is she afraid of us?" Katie asked.

"I don't think so," I said. "She just doesn't quite know what to make of all this."

"Poor thing," said Laura, who had planted herself on the floor behind Tasha.

"Well, I can see Tasha's going to have lots of attention from all you girls," said Mrs. Drummond, a large, round social worker who wore her long split ends pulled back in a low ponytail.

"We gonna love her from our heart," Lily promised.

It is with some reservations that I enter into this contract that commands us to care for, but not permanently attach to another human being. I hope Lily can hold it together when she has to give the babies back. I hope I can.

I wish my mother was around to give us advice, having been through the process of salvaging damaged children. She adopted Jimmy and me after we were taken away from our biological mother on grounds of neglect. The upstairs neighbor called police when she heard us crying for more than three hours straight and got no answer when she knocked on our door at 11 at night. When police came, they took us to the emergency room and learned we had fevers of 102 and 103. Our mother had gone out binge drinking in the middle of flu season, leaving us alone in our crib, caked in vomit and diarrhea. She had stocked our crib with several bottles of formula and some saltines. Everyone surmised that it likely wasn't the first time she had left us alone to go out partying, but on all those other nights, our temperatures had been normal and we'd slept clear through until morning. It wasn't until I had children that I began to understand how depraved a mother would have to be to do what our biological mother did. And it wasn't until I had taken care of my *sick* children that I knew the full extent of her moral corruption. All I can figure is she must have been in some fast-falling spiral. She must have held us and fed us and comforted us at some point in the beginning, or else, as all the research shows, we wouldn't have been able to bond with anyone throughout our lives. And bond we did with our adoptive mother, Jen Eagan. Although, considering the type of person our mother was, it might have been impossible not to bond.

****

"Mom, have you seen my brown sandals, you know, the strappy ones with the big heel?"

"No, Babe, I'm sorry," I said. "Just wear your flats. I saw them in the downstairs bathroom. They'll be more comfortable to walk in anyway."

Laura's life reads like an *I Spy* book. Gold Challenge edition. Her room looks like someone intentionally planned to get as much unrelated stuff as possible into a given amount of space, so as to challenge the acuity of the eye. Could be something as small as a tube of chap stick or as large as a pair of jeans, but she seems genuinely perplexed when she can't find it. I've offered her alternatives. I've bought her crates, canvas cubes, shelving and labels. I've helped her organize and sort. Within 30 days, it's all back in the heap again. Meanwhile, some of the crates are empty, while others are filled with dirty clothes that have been MIA since the first or second time they were worn.

The rest of us are not neat freaks nor are we obsessive compulsive. We just have a threshold. We all have a different one, but we all have one. When the mess gets too much for us, we clean it up. Laura has no such threshold. I'm always impressed that Lily's threshold is the lowest of all of us. She will not abide a single item out of place. I remember Auntie Bev used to have to bribe or threaten her to do almost everything, including pee. But she never had to ask Lily twice to pick up her things. Lily would cheer for herself each time she tossed a toy in the box and then hum an off-pitch tune as she returned the box to the shelf. There was a bit of a spring in her step after.

Laura's big-heeled shoes were found under her bed, just in the nick of time. I had loaded Tasha in the car and had threatened to leave without her if she didn't just grab any pair of shoes and come on. I know Laura had a certain vision in her head of what she would look like pushing Tasha's stroller. We were going to the mall, not because we needed to buy anything, but because we needed to show Tasha off. The girls and Lily argued over which outfit to dress her in. I had to settle it with my veto power. She wore a peach-colored dress with a large white daisy on the front and a matching flop hat of white and peach stripe. Jake looked up from his game long enough to give the girls the desired approval of Tasha's outfit and wish us a good time. Even Beth wanted to come on this family outing. She never misses a trip to the mall. She would probably hitch a ride with a band of terrorists to get there. But since there were no terrorists on the way to the mall on this particular day, she had to go with us.

Our choice of outfit for Tasha proved inspired. Female shoppers throughout the mall took the bait. The girls beamed with pride as people doted over Tasha.

"She our new baby," Lily told the shoppers. "We love her from our heart."

We set Tasha free at an indoor playground themed like a fairytale land. We sat on benches on the side, watching the frenetic flurry of small bodies, and Lily's large one, bouncing in and out and through the miniature tutor houses.

"Why is Tasha so small?" Beth asked. "She's smaller than that little baby over there who can't even walk yet."

"Her mother used drugs when she was pregnant," I explained. "Then when Tasha was born, she was so busy partying, she forgot to feed her."

"That's sad," said Beth. But it wasn't sadness on her face. It was more like horror. "How could anybody do that?"

"The drugs did it," I said. "That woman may never get her child back again. She very well could lose her forever. And one day, if she ever sobers up, that will mean something to her."

Beth looked down at her hands, picking at her cobalt blue nail polish, quiet for quite a while. I figured she was probably applying this maxim about drug use to herself. I was hoping anyway. I was hoping she'd figure out it was the drug that made her steal from her sister and stay out all night without calling her distraught parents. And will one day make her barter her dignity for a "high" in the flea-infested bed of some two-bit drug dealer -- if it hasn't already.

****

I stood squinting at a label at half past 1 in the morning. I was squinting partly because the light was too bright for the middle of the night and partly because the expiration dates are always written in letters too small for the over-40 human eye. I couldn't believe virtually everything behind that medicine cabinet's mirrored door was expired. We moved so quickly that I didn't bother to sort this stuff out before we packed, so we ended up paying for a semi to haul boxes full of useless items halfway across the country. And so, in the middle of the night, I read labels. There was the Codeine given after Katie's tonsillectomy. Could that really have taken place more than three years ago? Benadryl that is three months past expiration. I wondered if I should keep that? I'll throw it away after I get new, I guess. The drops for earaches, which we thankfully haven't had to use for at least two years. Children's Tylenol that expired last year. Antibiotic eye ointment for the scratched cornea, two years expired. I remember each of these remedies as if I'd used them yesterday. And yet, I have proof right here in my hands, in the form of expiration dates, that years have passed. For mothers, the passage of time is tallied more by triumphs, trials and wear and tear than by calendars, which we rarely have time to look at anyway. The falling out of baby teeth, the growing in of permanent ones. The disassembling of cribs and the passing on of car seats. The purchasing of training bras. The growing distance between pant hems and ankles, mother and child. The steady fraying of ropes on hammocks. The appearance and reappearance of rust stains in toilets. The annual reminders that it's time again for a mammogram. Hair that has grown literally behind our backs when we weren't looking, falling to the beauty shop floor, parting us from inches of our past and the pregnancy hormone that thickened and strengthened it. Were it not for such things -- and the expiration dates in medicine cabinets -- mothers would scarcely notice that time is passing. Other people will tell you that your children are growing like weeds, but you don't really notice, until one day, you're looking up into their eyes.

Finally, I found a bottle of children's cold medicine that was not outdated. Tasha was stirring and intermittently whimpering in her crib after a late night of coughing, crying, tugging at her ears, sucking her thumb, sniffling and finally drifting off to sleep while I rocked her in my arms. I wanted to make sure I was prepared with a dose of relief if she were to fully awake. My muscles were aching from lack of rest and I had that heavy pinch behind my eyes. I always prefer to get sick before my kids, so I can be more sympathetic to what they have. Getting sick after only gives you retroactive empathy, which isn't nearly as useful to them.

After checking Tasha's head for fever, I returned to my room, lay down in my bed and listened to the soft moans coming over the baby monitor. I was hoping it would subside so I could join Jake in a deep sleep. Then came a hushed voice that was not Tasha's.

"It's OK, Baby. Here, come here, Baby. Come with me." I heard rustling of sheets and blankets. "Here, let's bring your sippy cup."

Footsteps in the hallway, mixed with more whimpering, and then I heard nothing more. After a few minutes, I got up, tiptoed down the hall and found Tasha cozied into Beth's bed. Beth had propped the both of them up on double pillows and had wrapped her arms around the sick child, who was now resting peacefully with "face blanket," Tasha's dingy frays of pink fleece she brought with her when she came to live with us. We call it "face blanket" because Tasha holds it to her face to soothe herself to sleep.

I smiled as I made my way back down the hall, looking in at Katie and then Laura, sleeping like angels in their beds, probably dreaming of goats and tornadoes, disco balls and Mango Tango lip gloss.

Pablo Puppy was nestled in with Lily. An overwhelming torrent of love rushed into me, filling my chest so full I felt I would explode. As I steadied my back against the hallway wall, a tear splashed onto my toe. I crossed my hands over my heart and took deep breaths, crying and smiling -- almost laughing. I wanted to wake up Jake and tell him what a great family we have. But I knew it would be pointless to disturb his sleep. He already knew it. What I ought to do, I reasoned, is fling the windows wide open and scream it to the neighborhood. "I LOVE THESE PEOPLE! THESE ARE THE BEST CHILDREN IN THE WORLD! AND GOD HELP ME IF I SPEND ANOTHER DAY IN ANYTHING SHORT OF IMPASSIONED AWE!"

I went to the window in the study and looked out. A cat splotched with gray and white patches was casually crossing the road, tail down but bowed slightly up, paws padding lightly on the shiny wet pavement. Other than him, there was not a single soul in sight. Last night, I would have looked upon the street-lit emptiness of 2 a.m. and thought, "My, it is a lonely world out there." But tonight, I felt nourished and nurtured by its lavish generosity. I was insanely in love.

****

"Mommy, I have a stormy nose," Tasha said, wiping an abundance of mucous on her upper arm. It was, of course, only moments after taking her first bath in four days.

"I know," I said, giggling. "I'll get you a Kleenex."

Even when under the weather, Tasha is never off her game. She is the most poetic 3-year-old on the planet. I will have to say, poetry helps mitigate the drudgery of mothering.

Katie stayed home sick today, presumably with the same bug Tasha has had. After yet another full day of wiping nostrils, checking temperatures and dosing out medications, I was desperate for some time alone. At 9:15 p.m., I finally had a moment, and I just knew something was going to mess it up. Most likely, it was going to be Tasha. (She has been waking up every two hours or so ever since coming down with the virus, wanting a pat on the back or a drink of water to fall back to sleep. Sometimes she cries for Beth and it takes me a full 20 minutes to convince her that I'm not going to wake another member of the household to come and console her when I myself am perfectly capable.) I sat there on the toilet with *A Tree Grows in Brooklyn*, a book Auntie Bev passed down to me from her collection. In this new house, we are fortunate to have an extra room, which has become Jake's office and my study, lined from ceiling to floor with the books Auntie Bev treasured more than any of her children or grandchildren probably ever will, But I am willing to take a crack at it as I sit alone on the toilet. I was too nervous to savor the silence, because I knew it was bound to be broken. I listened hard to it, paying no attention to the words I was reading. And then, sure enough I heard it, a tiny, far-off squeak. Then another and another. Then, I realized it was my own nose. It occasionally squeaks when I exhale. Or maybe more than occasionally, but I'm sure it's usually drowned out by the din of chaos in this house. What mother can say she ever hears the sound of her own breath? She hears her husband's whoosh into her ear during times of passion or rattling her head when he's in deep sleep. She listens for her children's as she tiptoes into their rooms in the middle of the night to assure herself one last time that they are well. I still vaguely remember the strange sound Lily's breath would make when she was an infant. It was a loud squeak at each inhale, the way you might imagine someone would sound if they needed a tracheotomy. Just like the rest of her, Lily's windpipe was very floppy for the first year of her life. The doctor assured Mom that it was not a dangerous condition, although it sounded horrible, and that she would grow out of it. Mom was so accustomed to the noise coming from the bassinet by her bedside that, in the rare moments when Lily's breathing didn't sound labored, the strange silence would wake Mom up. Similar to how a man will wake up when you turn off the football game he's fallen asleep in front of.

****

Turns out Tasha slept through the night, but I was so nervous about her waking up that I didn't. Morning came far too soon, bringing with it the sounds of re-energized youth.

"Tasha, where's Tasha?" It was a song more than a question. The floor length curtains appeared to have grown two little pink feet. Hide and seek is one of Lily's and Tasha's favorite games. Lily is more a playmate to Tasha than a care giver. And because of that, she is Tasha's favorite. I learned when my kids were little that the person who gets down on the floor and plays with a child is the one who holds a special place in that child's heart. Those people are like dessert in a child's life. The Mom is the main course and the most vital, of course. But who would want to live in a world without dessert? I thought with so many girls in this house to take care of a little one, I might for once get to be somebody's dessert. But I guess I'd forgotten how much work a toddler is. When we signed up, we envisioned fostering a newborn. But the first call we got was about an almost 3-year-old in need of a placement that would more than likely be permanent. Although 3-year-olds wear you ragged, I didn't want to say no. And I figured we had enough people in this house to chase after one.

"Now you hide, Lily." Tasha does not make requests. She makes demands. And you will deliver -- if you know what's good for you. Lily ran off down the hall to the bathroom, presumably to hide behind the shower curtain.

Tasha noticed I had come downstairs and made a beeline to my leg as she suddenly remembered a new unvoiced ailment.

"I have a gas bubble," she said, boring her face into my thigh as I scuffed towards the coffee pot.

"You have a gas bubble?"

"Yeah, in my leg." She was scratching a mosquito bite on her shin. "See?"

"Oh, yes," I said. "A buggy bit you."

"That's not nice," she declared. "I don't like itchy gas bubbles."

What most children refer to as "owies" or "boo boos," Tasha calls gas bubbles because one time when she had a stomach ache, I told her it was caused by a gas bubble.

"Can you give me some medicine?" she whined.

"I can put some baking soda on it."

"No," she protested. "Not on it. I want the drinking medicine."

"The drinking kind won't help a mosquito bite, Love."

"Well, I want some."

"Well, your itch will go away soon," I said. "Let's go wake up Beth."

"Yay!" And the itchy gas bubble was forgotten.

"Hey," Lily yelled from the bathroom. "You suppose to be finding me."

****

Beth looked especially pale and apathetic on the drive to school. An orange-haired boy dressed in black, with a fat silver chain hanging from his pocket, stared into our car as we pulled up to the curb.

"Are you OK, Honey?" I asked as Beth gathered her books from the floor between her feet. "Do you want to take the day off and just hang out? We could go for a big breakfast. Dad's home all day today. We could get him to watch Tasha, and you and I could have a nice day together. Maybe do some shopping."

"I have two tests today."

She made her way to a group of darkly-dressed youths loitering in the parking lot. I sat and watched her disappear into the horde of woe that is America's future and I wondered which one of those up-and-comers is her supplier.

When I picked her up from school, she was sitting alone on the curb next to her backpack. She was squinting as if concentrating on whatever garbage was flowing into her brain from her earbuds. Laura was at home sick, watching videos in the study, and I was glad to get Beth in the car by herself -- well, without another teen-ager anyway. I had a proposal for Beth. The stolen money was a sign to me that she was returning to her previous lifestyle. She had established connections -- or at least hoped to. I only knew of one way to pinch off her line of supply.

"Hey, Beth, how was your day?" I said. "How'd you do on your tests?"

"Beth! Beth! Beth!" Tasha yelled from the back seat, kicking both of her feet at once.

"Hi, Squirt," Beth said, settling into her seat. She leaned into the head rest, closed her eyes and adjusted her earphones. Beth has become highly skilled at filtering all input from her family through an ever-present, brooding veil of melancholy music.

When we got onto the highway, I asked Beth how she liked school.

"Don't," she said flatly.

"Mr. Grinch doesn't have any underwear," Tasha remarked from the back. "He just has a butt."

"So, there's nothing you like about it?" I asked Beth.

"What? The Grinch's butt?"

"No, school."

"Nope." She stared out her window.

"And he has a Christmas tree umbrella," said Tasha.

"There's got to be something, Beth," I said.

"Nope."

"Not one single solitary thing."

"Not one."

"Good."

She looked at me for the first time since she'd gotten into the car.

"How would you like to be home schooled?" I said.

She turned off the music. "What does that mean?"

"You can do your school work at home. Take some on-line classes. Maybe take some community college courses. Maybe drawing or art classes."

She shrugged. "OK." She turned her music back on.

That was easy. No lamenting over friends. No complaining about having to deal with her irrelevant mother all day. No made-up objections meant to mask her unwillingness to leave an established drug connection.

"It would be really great to have your help at home," I said. "With Tasha."

She shrugged again. "Sure," she said, nonchalantly, as if I'd just asked her to pass the salt.

My reason for adding this was two-fold. First, I didn't want her to think I was pulling her out of school to keep her away from drugs. I knew that would be a point of rebellion. Second, I knew that loving Tasha would change Beth. And there is no faster route to love than through service. I had heard somewhere that the more you serve, the more you love.

"Did his doggy get to eat the roast beast?" Tasha asked.

"What does the Grinch have to do with anything, Tasha?" Beth asked. "It's not even Christmas."

"Jingle cows, jingle cows. The cows come first, but jingle bells and Santa Claus doesn't." Tasha sang the rest of the way home. Beth rolled her eyes, turned off her music and smiled, watching the road straight ahead.

12

PAYBACK

Kitchen islands are never a good idea when you've got a child who gets a charge out of leading a chase. Every night Auntie Bev would chase Lily around the island, pajamas in one hand and wet face cloth in the other, until either Jimmy or I would team up to close in on her. Lily would be laughing hysterically at this point, but Auntie Bev was just too darned tired at the end of the day to find any humor in a child delaying bedtime in favor of a game of cat and mouse. I was pretty certain Lily had outgrown that phase, so a kitchen island fit nicely into our renovation plans. However, I didn't know when we undertook the remodeling that we would have a Tasha. She is a swift little mouse and very strategic. Jake is the only one who can outsmart her. He does it, during a commercial break, with a combination of speed and psyche-out moves, his eyebrows raised high and his grin broad, and when he finally catches her, he scoops her up with one arm and turns her upside down, while she giggles fanatically. This is her reward for making us work twice as hard to get her ready for bed. This is how you are treated as the youngest member of a family whose children are almost all grown. You are rewarded for things your elder siblings were reprimanded for.

"Come on, Tasha," I said. "We have to get up early tomorrow. You better get in bed."

It was another forty-five minutes of delays and stall tactics -
- including one trip to the bathroom, one to the linen closet to get
a lighter-weight blanket, one to the book shelf to exchange *If
You Give a Mouse a Cookie* for *Mr. Brown Can Moo*, and three
trips to the faucet. It's like children turn into camels at bedtime.
You'd think after all that, you'd have the decency to let your
parents get a good night's sleep. But no.

Tasha woke up in the middle of the night crying. Actually,
wailing.

"My baby elephant, my baby elephant," she mourned.
"They threw him in the lava pit! Those mean people threw my
baby elephant in the lava pit."

I felt so awful for her. In her mind, she had really lost a pet -
- in the cruelest of manners, no less. I just held her and told her it
was all a nightmare, but she didn't believe me. Eventually, sleep
took back over and she quieted herself into a sound sleep that
lasted the rest of the night. I was glad because a sleepless night
would mean a difficult morning. And this was one of those rare
Sunday mornings when I had to get everyone ready in real
clothes. We were going out to Queen of Peace for Mass.

Lily took a shower in my bathroom while I fixed my hair.
She was making butt prints and giggling at them. It's a skill I
taught her when we were kids. We would press our butts against
the glass shower door and then turn around and admire the heart
shapes created by the rubbed off steam. Lily would laugh so
hard, I would have to guard against her losing her footing and
falling in the slippery stall. Auntie Bev would get after us for
causing her extra scrubbing. But the making of butt prints was
particularly funny today because I got a look at it from the other
side of the shower door. I was laughing so hard I had to put my
curling iron down, for my lack of muscle control that would
surely get me burned. Lily laughed even harder. Hearing her reminded me that Mom used to call her Giggles. The nickname
was lost somewhere in the move to Auntie Bev's house.

After her shower, Lily brushed Katie's hair while Katie
brushed Tasha's. I was impressed by how gentle they both were.

No one was wincing with the pain of snagged tangles. Lily has brushed Katie's hair every day since we moved her in with us. Katie volunteered to grow her hair out when she learned that Lily missed combing Auntie Bev's. I've never seen hair as long as Auntie Bev's on a woman her age. I guess she didn't have the heart to take it away from Lily, who can't grow her own hair past her collarbones without it looking thin and straggly. I think Lily would have loved to have been a hair stylist, but hair is probably one of those things people wouldn't trust her with -- right up there with brain surgery. Most all people are fanatical about quality haircuts. Nobody I know takes risks with that. They will go to chef schools for lunch and they will let an intern examine them when they're brought in for chest pains to the emergency room. But when it comes to their hair, the stylist has to have come highly recommended by a trusted friend or relative who has an overwhelmingly positive good-hair day ratio.

****

The first thing I noticed about being back at church is the saying "Once a man, twice a child," is never more embodied than by the very old and very young who attend Mass.

The babies all have their sippy cups, chew toys, blankets and burp cloths laid out on the pew. The elderly have their water bottles, prayer cards, rosary beads, breviaries, bibles and tissues. Those between the ages of 7 and 67 show up empty-handed.

The second thing I noticed about Queen of Peace parishioners is that there are some true believers in their midst. A woman in her sixties, with flaming red hair and bright red lipstick lifted her hands in the air, waving them gently, eyes closed, head tipped back, singing "Glory to God." She was singing to someone -- someone very real and someone she loved without reserve. I had never sung like that before, but I wanted to. I wondered why some people feel things deeper than others.

Lily rested her head on my shoulder. I was immediately taken back in time to the Masses we attended as kids. She would always lay her head in my lap or Jimmy's. If she chose Jimmy's, he would softly stroke her hair. If she chose me, she would end up with a mini-braid, which she would press between her fore-finger and thumb and smile as if I'd just given her a complete makeover.

Beth held Tasha in her lap and let her look at the pictures on her cell phone to keep her quiet during the homily. I was won-dering what Beth was going to do during the consecration, when everyone is supposed to kneel. The last time we attended church, she just sat. She had an excuse not to kneel this time, given the toddler on her lap who might make trouble if she put her down. Beth scooted forward in her seat, still holding Tasha, making room for the person behind her to pray. Holding the golden cha-lice, Father Fitz said, "This is the blood of the new and everlasting covenant, which will be shed for you and for all so that sins may be forgiven. Do this in memory of me." He looked straight into Beth's eyes for just a moment, raised the chalice, set it on the altar and genuflected. Beth put Tasha beside her and kneeled. Tasha knelt also. For about twenty seconds. She spent the remainder of the consecration crawling along the pew behind everyone.

Father Fitz greeted us with hugs after Mass. He gave Tasha a blessing and a high-five for correctly answering his question about how many fingers he was holding up. "And that's how many persons are in the Blessed Trinity," he added. "Father, Son and Holy Spirit."

A game of tag broke out in the courtyard. Katie has always been one of the fastest runners in her class, but she was losing this game.

"Mommy, I can't run in these shoes," she said, still full of adrenalin, panting and grabbing me around the waist.

"I know, Katie," I said. "I haven't mastered that either."

It's not easy being 11. You finally convince your mother to buy you high heels and, although your feet look pretty, you real-ize it's going to be quite some time before your gait will. You spend hours surveying your stride in a full-length mirror, wanting to look like your older sister's cool best friend, but looking instead like a fawn, fresh out of its mother's womb, taking its first steps. Then, when you've finally mastered it, you find yourself in the unfortunate position of having chosen to wear them on a day when a spontaneous game of tag breaks out. And you sit with your Dad pretending you're too old for such games, but knowing you would give anything for a pair of flats right now. People get to a certain age and they just don't run anymore. Unless they are running on a treadmill or running to catch a train. They don't run and they don't play, so tag is out. But when you're 11, you're not ready for running to be over. So my advice to moms would be to deny their young girls high heels until they get a desk job.

"You got my letter, Beth?" Father Fitz asked.

"Uh-huh."

"You know, I spent eight years in seminary studying theology, striving to become the best priest I possibly could. I have made a life's work of studying the great thinkers, the great philosophers. Plato, Socrates, Aquinas, Augustine. But they never taught me what you did, Beth, with your pencil and a piece of paper and your God-given talent."

She stared out at the children playing, her eyes fixed on Tasha, who was darting through the throng like a billiard ball, tagging anyone she got close to, unaware that the game has a small but important set of time-tested rules.

"You know what you taught me?"

"No."

"Mercy has no bounds."

She glanced at Father and back at the kids.

"You are a prophet, my friend," he said. "A prophet with a pencil. And a very deep wound."

She looked at him, stunned, with questioning eyes.

"I'm a bit of a prophet too," Father said. "So we understand each other."

****

132

I hate loud noises in the morning -- unless they are coming from the coffee grinder or the espresso machine. But this morning, they were coming from a 3-year-old with a wet head. "I want my fat hair back!"

"Your what?"

"My fat hair," Tasha screamed. "Beth made my hair wet and now it's not fat anymore."

Beth rolled her eyes and shook her head. "All of a sudden, she doesn't like getting her hair washed," she said. "What's with that?"

"One of many phases to come," I said. "Next week she'll be dumping pitchers of orange juice over her head."

"I want my fat hair back!" Tasha insisted.

"It will come back when it dries," I said.

"I want it back *now*!"

"I've got to get dressed," Beth said. "I'll let you take over."

"Thanks," I said. "Come on, Tasha, let's go blow dry your hair."

"I don't want to," she said. "Too windy."

"OK," I said. "Let it dry on its own. But this *is* Seattle. It may be a while before you see your fat hair again."

Red-faced screaming. I got her settled down by promising a Disney princess DVD.

A half hour later, Laura bounded down the stairs. "Mom, I need to give this back to you." she held out a $100 bill, smiling.

"What's this?" I asked.

"The $100 you gave me to make up for the money Beth stole. She gave it back to me."

"She did?"

"Yeah. She admitted she stole it and gave it back."

"I want more toast," Tasha said.

"Eat your eggs," I told her.

Tasha was now seated at the kitchen table, wearing pink Sleeping Beauty pajamas and a glittery plastic tiara on shiny copper hair, slowly drying its way into ringlets. "If we eat our bread, we can be happy," she said, seeming to sense the chemical connection between carbohydrates and comfort.

"I thought Beth already got Tasha dressed," Laura said. "What's she doing back in her PJ's?"

"She's a princess," I said. "So what did you tell Beth?"

"About what?"

"The money."

"I told her I knew she stole it and thanks for finally giving it back."

"Did you forgive her?"

"Yeah, I guess so."

"Did you tell her that?"

"No. I don't really know if I forgive her."

"I know it's hard, Honey, but it's a huge thing for Beth to admit what she's done wrong and try to make it right."

"So she gets to make a bunch of bad choices and life just goes on as if nothing ever happened?"

"What should happen?" I asked.

"She doesn't even get punished for stealing?"

"We already knew she stole it," I said. "Now she's finally admitting it. I'm not going to punish her for that. She's been doing extra chores around here to earn money, and now we know why. Nobody told her to do that. She's trying to make amends, Laura. She wants her sister back."

She sat quietly for a minute looking down at her hands, which were fidgeting with a paper clip that had been lying on the counter. "OK," she said quietly.

"Here," I said, giving her the $100 back. "A reward for your honesty."

She looked puzzled.

"Some people would have just kept the money," I told her. "You decided to give it back to me. That's the kind of thing that makes me trust you. Always."

She hugged me. "Thanks, Mom."

I knew she was thanking me more for my trust than for the money. She lilted from the kitchen and turned as she got to the

stairs. "I'm going to go tell Beth right now that I forgive her."
It's amazing how a little extra cash can spawn such goodwill between sisters.

"Can I have some money?" Tasha asked. "I want some
money."

"Eat your eggs," I said. "We're going to the beach today."

"Can we bring bread?"

People are most emphatically themselves at the beach. I
have noticed this in my children. Beth was, from a very early
age, quite an accomplished swimmer, at least in still waters. We
will never know how she would have fared in the ocean. She
never could stand the seaweed wrapped around her ankles, so
she spent all our seaside vacations building castles and burying
her own limbs in the sand. Laura walked along the fringes of the
waves, collecting shells and harvesting seaweed for fashion,
weaving it into a primitive crown and wearing it in casual cas-
cades over her lush curls. Katie rushed headlong into the roaring
sea, never stopping to look back at the shore or anyone on it,
blind and deaf to the parents, too many paces behind her, franti-
cally waving her in, their voices swallowed up by the noisy tide,
their heads flooded with frightful images of the heartless waves
permanently gulping down the baby of the family. Katie has
never been a weigher of risks. If she deems something as fun she
will pursue it. For this reason, she was the child you had to explain things to in explicit detail, the kind of detail you would
have spared most young children so as not to leave them morti-
fied at the brutality of nature and human beings. I always figured
I'd rather scare the living daylights out of her than see her lose
her life. This, I imagine, is why she is so fascinated with devas-
tating forces, like tornadoes.

"Why don't dads need bathing suits?" Tasha asked, crunching into her third piece of toast.

"They don't?" I asked.

"No," she replied. "They jump in with their bellies."

"Eat your eggs, your highness."

13

PARTICIPATION POINTS

I had promised Beth that if she cleaned up her act, I'd help her get a driver's permit. I think I was happier than she was when I took her to the DMV last week. It meant that what I had viewed a year ago as unlikely, if not absurd, was now coming to pass.

Today, I let Beth drive to the park to pick up Lily from an outing with other mentally disabled people in a day program. The group was having a picnic, but Lily had to leave early to go to work. Beth did a fine job of driving. We arrived at the park a little early so we could let Tasha play for a bit. Beth made no protests about that, since she was so eager to drive.

When we got there, Lily was nowhere in sight. One of the chaperones told us the female contingent of their group had gone over to the volleyball courts and they were due to return shortly. The rest of the group was sitting around several picnic tables under a ramada finishing up their snacks. One man was skinny with no front teeth, except for his canines. I imagined his less than perfect smile had something to do with his refusal to brush his teeth.

"Cute kid," he said watching Tasha run off into the sand. "Cute kid."

"Thank you," I said.

"That's a cute kid," he said. "Cute kid."

"Thank you."

Tasha had found an abandoned shovel and was digging.

"What's her name?"

"Tasha," I said.

"What's your name?" he asked.

"Terry. What's yours?"

"I'm Lewis." He held out his hand. "Nice to meet you."

"Nice to meet you," I said.

"Hi," he held out his hand to Beth. "I'm Lewis. What's your name?"

"Beth," she said shaking his hand.

Lewis eyed the keys in her hand.

"Do you drive?" he asked. "I'm going to drive some day. I love cars. I love muscle cars. Do you like muscle cars?"

"They're OK, I guess," Beth shrugged.

Tasha came running up, with some news. "I saw an insect," she proclaimed.

"What insect was it?" I asked.

"A thing that sucks with a straw," she hollered, running off again. "A butterfly sucker."

"Cute kid," Lewis said as Tasha resumed a crouched position next to a flowering shrub. "Cute kid. How old is she?"

"Almost three," I said.

"When is her birthday?"

"July 4," I said.

"I'm 35. I'll be 36 on July 3. I'm 35 now. I'll be 36. How old are you, Beth?"

"15."

"Do you like Jack in the Box?"

"It's OK," she said.

"Is that your favorite?" I asked Lewis.

"Yeah. Jumbo Jack, fries and a drink. Jumbo Jack fries and a large drink."

"What drink do you like?" I asked.

"Root beer. Do you like root beer?"

"Oh, yes," I said. "It's one of my favorites."

"Me too. I like root beer. What about you, Beth? Do you like root beer?"

"Yeah," she was smiling now. "It's my favorite."

Lewis' smile widened. "Me too. Root beer is my favorite. You're a very nice kid, Beth. I think if I didn't live in a group home, I could be friends with you. But people like me, we don't have friends like people like you."

"Hi" a man with blonde hair parted down the middle called out from an adjacent picnic table. "Do you like music?"

"Oh yeah," said Beth.

"I love music," he said. "I like hard rock."

"Me too," Lewis said. "I love music."

A large, soft man with a confused look on his face, bent slowly to the ground to pick something up.

"Oh, Eddie," one of the chaperones said. "You and your bottle caps. Come here. Let me see what else you've collected."

The man ignored her and stooped to pick up something else.

"Come here, Eddie," she cajoled. "Let me see your pockets."

Eddie ambled over to her and opened his hand to reveal a small pink oleander bloom.

"Oh, that's a pretty flower," the woman said.

"Mommy," he said.

"Is that for your Mommy?" she confirmed.

Eddie nodded.

"That's very nice, Eddie," she said. "I don't know if that will last until Saturday. We may have to get another one to give her." She glanced over at me and raised one eyebrow. "If she shows up this time." She said that last part without opening her mouth too much, as if maybe Eddie can't hear so well but reads lips.

I felt a sharp pain of sorrow in my chest when she said it, and I wanted to cry for him.

The chaperone persuaded Eddie to show her the contents of his pockets -- three white water bottle caps and a green seed pod that had fallen or had been plucked from a lipstick tree.

"OK," she said. "That's OK. Nothing sharp."

While the chaperone explained to us that Eddie's pockets have to be cleaned out after every outing, Eddie tapped her on the shoulder and pointed to a ribbon tied to the leg of a picnic table, where a balloon had been tethered and cut off. For a junk collector like Eddie, it was a prize. He looked at her longingly.

"I know, Eddie," she said, pushing a straw into her drink box. "That's a ribbon. We can't get it. It's tied on."

He pointed at her straw and grunted.

"Straw. That's my straw, Eddie."

He studied it hard, like he'd seen one somewhere before, but just couldn't place it.

He pointed back at the ribbon.

"I know you want that, Eddie," she said. "But we can't get it off the table."

Tasha ambled up holding a shovel. She squatted down, her skinny pale knees pointing out from under her yellow gingham dress. She pressed her shovel onto the cement.

"I must mash them," she said. "If ants bite us, we must get owies."

Where most of us say "will," Tasha says "must."

A man in his late 20s with Down Syndrome walked by us to get a drink at the water fountain. On the way back, he stopped in front of us.

"Hi," he said, holding out his hand. I grasped it in a firm handshake.

"Get out of here," he said.

"David, that's not nice," the chaperone said. "Tell her you love her."

"I love you," David said.

"I love you too," I said.

"Get out of here," he said.

"His 17-year-old brother has been teaching him all kinds of words," the chaperone said. "He taught him how to do the bird, only David does it like this." She held her fingers in the shape of a gun and chuckled. "So I guess it's not all that bad."

While all this was going on, Eddie had somehow gotten the balloon string loose. He was holding it above his head, looking up at it in awe of its dangling disposition.

"Do you like Spider Man?" asked the one who had earlier asked about music. I couldn't tell if he was asking me or Beth because he had a wandering eye. "Do I look like Flash Thompson?"

I waited a few seconds for Beth to respond, but she didn't. "I don't know very much about Spider Man," I said. "What do you think Beth? Do you think he looks like Flash Thompson?"

"Kind of," she said. She glanced at me and shrugged.

"Thank you," he said, beaming. "Everybody says I look like Flash Thompson."

"I'm getting a job in four weeks," Lewis told me. "If I'm appropriate. I got to be appropriate."

"Where are you going to work?" I asked.

"I don't know. I got to be appropriate."

David, the one with Down Syndrome, put his head down on the table and wept.

"What's wrong David?" the chaperone asked.

"Hungry. Home," he said, his face contorted in misery.

"We'll go soon, David. It's time to play basketball first. Anyone who is finished eating can go to the court."

Several of the men slowly stood and made their way to the garbage can to deposit their trash before going to the court. David resumed his sobbing.

Lewis stayed behind, too.

"I never get it in the basket," he complained.

"That's OK," said the chaperone. "I can never get a basket either, but I keep trying so I can get better at it."

"But I don't know how," Lewis said.

"So, does this mean you won't be getting your participation points today?"

He stood up right away, with a smile on his face. "Oh, no," he said. "I'm getting my points. When I get 25, I'm going to buy a CD."

David was still bawling.

"David, go run," said the chaperone.

David immediately shut off the sobbing and ran toward the court, circling it round and round.

"There he goes," the chaperone said. "He runs everywhere. Runs all day."

Lewis had returned with more complaints that he couldn't get the ball into the basket.

"Well, Lewis, that's OK," said the chaperone. "I'm proud of you because you tried. That's what counts."

Lily came back from the volleyball courts with four of her friends.

"Everybody," she announced, "that my sister and my niece. My niece drives."

"What's her name?" asked a tall, slender woman staring into Beth's face.

"That Beth," Lily said. "She got a shrink just like you. But she not crazy like you." Lily elbowed her in the ribs and grinned.

"Lily," I said. "We've got to go or you'll be late for work."

I gathered Tasha in from the sand. Lewis once again told us how cute Tasha is.

"Can I talk to your kid?" he asked Beth.

"Sure," she said, shrugging. "But she's not my kid."

Tasha hid behind my leg as Lewis tried to get close to her face and say good-bye.

"She's a little shy," I said.

"Come on, Lewis," the chaperone said.

"Cute kid, Beth" he said. "Take care of that kid."

David had started to run onto an adjacent court, threatening to disrupt a game.

"Come on, David," the chaperone called. "Come on."

David just kept running.

The other chaperone, who had come back with the women playing volleyball, gave it a try. "David," she called out. "Come here, David." She held her arms out wide. He noticed her, changed directions and flew into her arms.

On the way home, after dropping Lily off at work, Beth was her normally quiet self until we pulled into our neighborhood.

"Do you think that's true what he said?" she asked, staring at the windshield. "That they only have friends in the group home."

"I don't think so," I said.

"I would be his friend," said Beth. "If I could."

14

AN END UNTO HIMSELF

Lily likes to set up elaborate scenes with the dolls she has saved from her childhood. She has one of mine, too, from when I was a little girl. I gave it to her when I went away to college. Today, Lily's dolls were all in school before the majority of us had woken up. They sat in a row, facing Lily, each with a Dr. Seuss book. They were learning to read. While Lily took care of the academics, she put Tasha in charge of preparing their snacks, taking them to the bathroom and watching them at recess. I guess that would make Tasha the teacher's aide.

"Why did Theo chew my doll's head off?" Tasha asked Lily, while handing out boxes of raisins. Tasha doesn't talk much about her past. She doesn't talk about family members at all, except for an occasional mention of a very big dog named Theo.

"I don't know," Lily said, unpacking an assortment of doll clothes from a Sleeping Beauty backpack. "That's not a good dog."

"Why do dogs have sharp teeth?" Tasha asked.

"To chew their food," Lily said.

"And dolls."

"I guess so," Lily shrugged, forcing a doll arm into a sweater sleeve.

"But Pablo Puppy doesn't chew my dolls," Tasha said. "He's a nice dog. Everyone here is nice. Nobody is mean to my doll."

"Yeah, Pablo Puppy a nice dog. My Daddy gave him to me."

"Please I feed Pablo Puppy tricks?" Tasha asked.

"OK." Lily went to the pantry and pulled out a box of Milk Bone biscuits. Pablo Puppy leapt at her knees in anticipation. Lily handed the box to Tasha and the dog forwarded his attentions to the small curly-headed girl, whose entire arm was engulfed by the box.

"Don- give him too many," Lily warned. "He get sick and barf."

That is not outside the realm of possibilities. Yesterday, an opened carton of eggs fell to the floor. Eggs are not among the easiest messes to clean up, so I decided to let Pablo Puppy help me. Then, he jumped up on Lily's bed and threw up all over the *Highlights* magazine joke page. Which made one immediately come to mind. "What did the Mom say to the *Highlights* joke page after the dog barfed an egg on it? The yoke's on you." Any kid would love that one. Maybe I'll send it in.

In fact, maybe I'll give up cooking and go into joke writing. Nothing I do in the kitchen comes out right lately. Last week, I forgot the eggs in the brownie mix. The kids said they were the best brownies they ever had. The other day, I mixed up a Texas sheet cake, popped it in the oven and then had the sinking feeling that I had forgotten to add the baking soda. I was about ready to start over again when I noticed some white powder on the measuring spoon. It tasted salty, so I assumed it was baking soda. I had absolutely no memory of adding it. I have had to live my life lately on clues. Like, sometimes I have to sniff my hair to make sure I remembered to use shampoo. I was on the internet at 2 a.m. this morning looking up early Alzheimer's. I hate to think what it would mean to my family. Auntie Bev's mind was sharp to the very end, which was a blessing. It's hard enough dealing with physical disabilities, but mental impairment in someone who used to take care of you is yet again a whole other tragedy.

But life is full of those. I called everyone together this evening after dinner and told them Tasha was leaving us. A paternal grandmother had surfaced a few months ago and she has fulfilled all the requirements to adopt Tasha. Laura ran and shut herself in her room. Katie -- not a crier, you'll remember -- burst into tears and ran to Tasha, who was sitting in the middle of the family room floor playing with her little people. Katie threw her arms around Tasha, who warded her off with a shrug that revealed that she was, at that moment, more interested in the imaginary lives of plastic people than the affections of real ones. Lily walked solemnly to Tasha and sat down on the floor with her, frowning silently. She patted her on the head and said "I gonna miss you, Tasha, but I promise to visit you every day."

"OK," said Tasha. I had told her earlier that she was going to go live with her grandma and she seemed fine with it, though I don't know if she understands permanency. I don't think she knows that she will probably not see us again -- unless her grandmother is generous about us visiting once in a while.

Beth just watched the whole thing unfold. Finally, she proclaimed, "This sucks," and got up from her place on the third step, where she sat during family gatherings, her way of making a statement that she was only partly with us. "Why does life always have to suck?" she mumbled.

Since she was already halfway up the stairs when she asked it, I assumed it must have been a rhetorical question. I was glad, too, because I wouldn't have known how to answer that one. A few moments later I heard loud, depressing music coming from her room.

I sent Laura upstairs to deliver the message that we were going for ice cream. Even Jake was coming with us. That's how grave this situation was. Growing up, that's always how our family drowned sorrows -- or smothered them, or whatever would be the correct terminology for asphyxiation by ice cream. I remember in the days immediately following our mother's death, Auntie Bev would come home with a half gallon of Breyer's. She would take two spoons out of the drawer and give them to me and Jimmy. We would sit on the towel-covered couch and eat out of the carton together. It might have been Rocky Road or strawberry or pistachio. She would set Lily up at the kitchen table with a bowl of vanilla ice cream, giving her the "special" spoon, which was a long red one Auntie Bev had once saved after eating a Dairy Queen Blizzard. She was able to convince Lily, at least for a while, that she was the privileged one. In reality, Lily got vanilla because Auntie Bev hated messes, and white ice cream made for considerably easier clean-up than brown or pink or green.

On the way to the ice cream parlor, Lily sat on one side of Tasha and Laura and Katie fought over who was going to sit on the other. They know their time with her is limited, and any limited commodity -- be it pizza or proximity to a toddler -- can disrupt the tenuous harmony that pretends to exist between siblings. Beth had originally said she didn't want to go, but I promised her a trip to the mall this weekend if she did. I don't know why the promise of ice cream is not enough to make you want to go out for ice cream, but with Beth, nothing can be easy.

****

The case worker was about as welcomed as a pitted prune. None of us had it in us to show Mrs. Drummond any kind of hospitality. And even though we knew this grief she was bringing was not her fault, there was nothing we could find to like about her. She told us in a professionally detached tone that she realized it must be hard what we're going through. Her empathetic sentiments notwithstanding, we chose to hate her because we had to have someone to hate.

Tasha bawled the loudest I'd ever heard, wrapped her arms around my neck in a death grip and screamed, "No, I don't want to go. I don't want to!" Mrs. Drummond calmly explained things, but Tasha buried her head in my hair and was unwilling to hear any of it.

"I don- wan- her to go!" Lily wailed, wrapping her arms around me and Tasha.

"Lily, Honey, remember we talked about this," I told her. "We have to let Tasha go to her forever family. That's where we all belong -- with our forever family."

"I wan- her forever," Lily cried.

"This is really not helpful," Mrs. Drummond said. "Maybe Lily should excuse herself from the room, so we don't upset Tasha even more."

I could not believe this woman was trying to deny Lily the grief of losing something so precious. Based on what happened next, I presume mine wasn't the only blood approaching boiling point.

"Maybe you should excuse *your*self," Beth said to Mrs. Drummond, putting her arm around Lily. "You suck every bit as much as your stinking system."

"Beth!" I exclaimed.

Jake stood silently with a hand on each of his youngest daughter's shoulders. Laura and Katie just looked on in shock and sadness, as if all of this was happening without warning. I had tried to prepare them for this since the day Tasha came to live with us. But even I was astounded at the brutal sorrow of this moment.

"Here, let me talk to her," said Beth, lifting Tasha's arms away from my neck. "Come here, Squirt."

Tasha detached herself from me and transferred her death grip to Beth's neck.

"Listen," said Beth, patting her back and bouncing her. "You have to go for just a little while, but we're going to come see you soon, OK? And maybe you can come and see us, too."

Tasha had entered into the kind of breathless hysteria that children spiral into when their world is crashing down around them, either because they have been denied a box of chewy double-dipped rainbow Nerds at a grocery store checkout stand or because they are being ripped away from the only family they can remember having.

"We better go," said the social worker. "It's time." She unfastened Tasha from Beth's neck, which was marked with red splotches from the tiny girl's attempt to permanently fuse herself onto our lives.

We spent the afternoon crying, except Beth, of course. She just slammed as usual. The sun set on a house full of females who had no tears left to cry, so we ate Cheetos and ice cream while watching sit-coms. Beth finally came out of her room and joined us. Jake emerged from his office, offering to pick up take out, but we told him not to bother, that we were not hungry. We proceeded to gorge ourselves on fat, salt, MSG, sugar and carrageenan.

****

I awoke this morning not remembering that Tasha was gone. Within about two minutes, it hit me like I was learning it all over again. The idea sickened me and I had to run to the toilet and throw up. I had a vague queasy feeling up until early afternoon. I wish I wasn't the type who lived my life out through my stomach. Many of us woman are like that. Or it could have been the junk food. The girls' stomachs weathered it all much better than mine, owing to their youth, I guess.

Katie's method was to go for the hair off the dog that bit her.

"Mom, when were Pringles invented?" she wanted to know as she packed her lunch.

"Before me," I said.

"How do they make them?"

"I don't know."

"They're odd," she observed, putting one close enough to her face to make her eyes cross. "They have these tiny bumps that are all the same."

"Processed."

"What are those bumps?"

"Pieces of dried potato, reconstituted, shaped, formed and pressed."

"Why don't they just slice a potato and fry it?"

"Why do you always ask for Pringles instead of Ruffles?"

"Because I like Pringles."

"Well, that's why they do it." I tried to take a swig of my coffee, but the smell of it steaming from the cup made my stomach turn before I got it to my lips. "Are you going to pack something healthy, Katie? Maybe an apple or some carrots?"

"I guess so," she said cheerfully.

I called Lucy Rowley to tell her I wouldn't be coming to the meeting. I hadn't even done the reading yet anyway. Later in the day, I felt better and opened the book to John Paul II's *Letter to Families*.

God willed man from the very beginning, and God wills him in every act of conception and every human birth. God wills man as a being similar to himself, as a person. This man, every man, is created by God for his own sake. That is true of all persons, including those born with sicknesses or disabilities. Inscribed in the personal constitution of every human being is the will of God, who wills that man should be, in a certain sense, an end unto himself ... To be human is his fundamental vocation: to be human in accordance with the gift received, in accordance with that "talent" which is humanity itself, and only then in accordance with other talents.

A torrent of joy rushed through me as I read. This truth -- abridged by the lofty intellect of a brilliant theologian -- puts words to the certainty I discovered at age 11, when Lily ate my science experiment. And then, after the joy, came a sudden and intense anger, sweeping through me like a back draft. I couldn't believe that case worker would be so cold as to suggest that Lily should leave the room -- that her emotions were discardable and ignorable. I have no scientific evidence to prove this, of course, but I think people like Lily have emotions that run deeper than the rest of us. I just remember how much more intense all my feelings were as a child. I don't think Lily has ever lost that.

The phone rang just after 1 p.m. I was about ready to put a soda cracker in my mouth. Lily was calling to ask if I'd pick her up. Mr. McCrae was sending her home early. She couldn't stop crying, and it was depressing the customers.

I picked her up and hit the drive-through. The smell wafting out the window as I paid for the food was too much for me, but it was nothing compared to the ride home. I had to roll the windows down.

"Can we go see Tasha?" Lily asked, sticking her hand into the paper sack.

"Not today," I said.

"Why?"

"She's settling in at her new place," I said.

Lily dropped whatever she had grasped inside the bag and put both hands over her face. Tears began to flow anew.

"Oh, Lily, it's OK," I said patting her on the arm. "Maybe they'll let us visit her soon."

For dinner, I made her other favorite meal. Every time I make scrambled eggs, I think of Don Simon. I remember how he used to stir them too much, too often. They would get mushy and mealy, instead of retaining a nice rolling landscape of large solid lumps. I always saw his over-attended eggs as a character flaw.

****

My nausea returned this morning. I had a really hard time getting out of bed. Fortunately, Beth took over my morning duties. I think I must have a bug. It has zapped all of my energy and now I'm pretty sure it's not just a junk food hangover or an emotional response to Tasha's departure. Beth made breakfast for everyone and cleaned up the kitchen afterwards. Even after paying Laura back, she has continued to do odd jobs around the house to earn money. I had been reluctant to give her any money because of the way she may spend it. But now that she's home schooled, I pretty much have all of her minutes accounted for. There's not much opportunity to stray into the hands of drug

150

dealers when you never go out of the house without a family member. I think she's rounded a corner anyway. She's done a lot of growing up in the past year, due in part to learning how to step outside herself into the pain of someone who needed her. I have to admit I was somewhat impressed at the way she nearly took that caseworker's head off. The old Beth would have stood by brooding, mumbling obscenities about the woman under her breath. Her aggressive approach isn't exactly my style, but it was refreshing to witness her role as Mama bear, showing her teeth for the welfare of someone other than herself.

Tasha was so good for us. We will never call a vacuum cleaner a vacuum cleaner again. It will henceforth be the "sucker-upper thing." I spent the day in my bathrobe thinking of all the adorable things Tasha would say and do. She has changed us forever.

This morning, after bringing me unsolicited dry toast and black tea, Beth asked me when was the next time I was going to my meeting at Queen of Peace. I told her it would be a couple of weeks.

"Why do you ask?" I said.

"I have something to give to Father Fitz," she said.

"Oh, OK," I said. "Another drawing?"

"No," she said.

"What is it? If you don't mind my asking."

She handed me an envelope, thick with cash.

"You're giving him a donation?"

"For the orphanage."

I remembered that Father had mentioned an orphanage in his homily. He had gone to Haiti on a mission when he was first ordained and had been raising support for the orphanage there ever since. I didn't realize Beth was even listening.

"Kind of a tribute to Tasha," Beth said as I handed the envelope back to her. "I don't know what else to do."

"Maybe we can go to Mass Sunday and give it to him."

"Yeah, OK," she said.

Yes, Tasha was very good for us. And we were good for her.

Although she hardly ate a thing when she first came to us, she'd acquired a hearty appetite by the time she left. Three bites into her meal, she'd put us on warning that it was not going to be enough -- always in the form of a question.

"Can you cut some more? Can you make some more? Can you buy some more?" In other words, please let there be an endless supply of this stuff I love so much.

She was a different child when she left. She was plump in mind and body.

****

I don't know if we'll make it to Mass this Sunday, after all. This morning I scuffed through the drug store, a gallon-sized Zip-loc bag in my purse, just in case I didn't make it to the toilet in time to throw up. It's been more than a decade since I needed a pregnancy test, and I wasn't sure where they keep them. I asked a teen-aged, freckle-faced boy who was wearing a tag that said, "Hello, how may I help you? My name is Rick," and I thought he should go by "Richie" because he looked so much like Richie Cunningham, except his teeth were very messed up. I imagined he was probably earning money for braces. I don't know why I was thinking all this about a stranger at a time like this, except that I was trying to picture what it would be like to have a teenage son.

When I got home, Beth was waiting for me to help her with her algebra. I wanted to bolt straight into the bathroom, but I knew I'd better help her first, since it was already after 10 and we hadn't gotten any school work done yet. I knew I'd have to take time to read the directions on the pregnancy test, so I decided to get her math lesson done first. The suspense was killing me, though, and it was very hard to care about solving for unknowns when the possibility of such a potentially huge change remained undisclosed to me.

"Look, Honey," I said. "If A + B = 72 - B3 and A = 24, then what do you do first?"

"I have no idea," Beth said.

I put my head in my hands and drew a long breath. "Me neither," I said. "Let's not do math today." I closed the book and stood up. "I have to pee."

****

I fixed Jake a lunch plate with a corned-beef sandwich and a pickle spear and brought it to his office. I couldn't eat, so I sat in the recliner across from his desk and watched him woof it down.

"Honey, you know how you said you miss having a little knucklehead around?" I said as he wrapped his mouth around the second half of the sandwich.

"Uh-huh."

"Did you really mean it?"

"Yes?" he said, turning toward me and suspiciously halting his chewing. "But I have to admit the quiet isn't bad either." He resumed his chewing and then took another bite.

"Uh-huh. I know what you mean," I said casually. "In a way." I picked up a *Sports Illustrated* -- the first one in his wrack -- turning pages and gazing straight through them as if through cellophane. "What would you say to having another little knucklehead?"

"Honey, I thought we agreed we were going to take a break. Did the caseworker call again so soon? I know it's hard to tell her 'no,' but..."

"No, not the caseworker," I said. "A higher source. And I can't tell Him no."

"Less cryptic please."

"The vasectomy reversal worked."

"What? I thought--" He put the sandwich down. "Are you kidding?"

"No."

"Wow," he said. "Wow. That's -- well, that's -- amazing."

"Yeah, I guess it is sort of amazing," I said, smiling.

Jake smiled back, rolled his chair over to my recliner and put his arm around me. "So that explains all the barfing."

"That explains it." It also explains why I have no memory. Pregnancy brain is what I called it with the last three.

"Huh. Imagine that," Jake said, shaking his head in disbelief. "We're having a baby. Do the kids know?"

"No, I thought you ought to be the first to know."

"Thank you," he said, standing over me and pulling me up by my hands. "Let's not tell anyone until Lily gets home."

"OK," I said, internally reeling from the magnificence of the man I married. "We'll wait until dinner.'

He took me in his arms and then moved his hand to my belly. A wave of warmth rushed through me at the very spot he touched. "When is the little guy due, Babe?"

"The little guy?" I said. "How do you know that?"

"Father's intuition, Babe," he whispered into my ear, hugging me tight with both arms.

"I'm not sure when he *or she* is due," I said. "I'm going to see the doctor Tuesday."

He held me in silence for several minutes.

"You seem happy, Honey," I said finally.

"I am," he said. "I didn't submit my nuts to the knife for nothing."

"That's profound," I said, dryly.

"That's not all," he said.

Here comes another smart alec comment, I assumed.

"It means the love of my life will have more love in her life." He smiled and winked and his beauty poked at my insides, causing sharp pleasurable pains in my gut. They were pains I hadn't felt in more than fifteen years.

15

NAUTICAL NURSERY

We decided we'd better wait until after my doctor's appointment to tell everyone. The doctor was able to determine that I am six weeks along and the baby is due March 31. He, of course, ordered the most advanced prenatal tests, which I declined.

"It's really advisable, Mrs. Lovely, given the advanced maternal age," he urged. "Being over 40 really heightens the risks of chromosomal abnormalities."

"If there's an abnormality we'll find out when the baby comes out," I said.

"OK, Mrs. Lovely. That's your prerogative, of course. We'll just have you sign a form that acknowledges that we recommended the tests and you declined."

"That's fine."

I know why that policy exists. I remember hearing about a blind and deaf woman in Australia who brought a "wrongful life" suit against the doctor who failed to diagnose her mother with Rubella while she was pregnant. She claims her mother would have aborted her if she had known, since Rubella can cause serious damage to the fetus. Then there was the couple who sued a doctor for failing to diagnose their 4-year-old daughter with Down Syndrome before she was born. They said they would have aborted her if they had known their daughter was carrying an extra chromosome.

Jake and I agreed to reveal our little surprise after dinner.

Lily jumped up and down in the middle of the family room, screaming "Yeah, yeah, yeah, yeah!" Laura and Katie joined her in the jubilation, holding hands and jumping together. Then the three of them clasped hands and danced around in a circle like revelers at the wedding of Motel and Tzeitel. Beth smiled quietly, came and sat down next to me and gave me a hug.

"Congratulations, Mom," she said, laying her head on my shoulder.

Jake snapped a picture of Lily kissing my belly. He printed it out and gave it to Lily, who immediately placed it in her photo album. Then she thumbed through the pages, smiling at the memories of her past.

"I haven't seen that album," I said. "Can I take a look?"

"Sure." Her smile widened at the idea of sharing her memories with someone interested enough to ask.

"This is me and Gwenny on the beach," Lily said. "I miss her." Gwenny, Lily's best friend, moved away to Los Angeles with her family just before Auntie Bev died.

I studied the photo of the two women with Down Syndrome sitting in the sand, feet stretched straight out in front of them, one of them holding her white floppy hat on so the wind wouldn't make off with it. It reminded me of the picture of Mom and Auntie Bev at the beach when they were little girls. Lily and Gwenny had the same squinty smiles, soft with the peace that a day with nature brings to children and the child-like. Lily turned another page and began to explain something about one of the photos.

"Wait a minute," I interrupted. "Who's this woman?"

"That's Agnes. She one of my friends at the nursing home. She in Heaven with Auntie Bev."

"Jake," I screamed. "Jake!"

He came running round the corner so fast, he nearly slammed shoulder first into the door. "What is it, Terry? What's wrong?"

"We're having a boy!" I screamed.

"What? How do you know?" He looked down at my belly for some kind of clue.

"Agnes told me."

"Who on earth is Agnes?"

I picked up the photo album and pointed wildly at a picture of Lily beaming between Auntie Bev and another elderly lady in a wheelchair.

"This is Agnes," I said pointing at the woman with the tartan green and blue plaid throw draped over her lap. "This woman came to me in a dream and brought our son to me."

I'm sure Jake chalked it all up to pregnant woman's hysteria. But I'm as certain as I can be that this soul I carry within me has his very own angel, and her name is Agnes.

****

We decided to have the attic finished off to make another bedroom. Beth will be choosing her color scheme this weekend. I'm hoping for anything other than black. Attics just don't seem to lend themselves to the dark and moody. We'll be re-doing Beth's room for the baby. Lily and I decided to go with a nautical theme. This will be the first Lovely child to grow up by the ocean.

"If you want to ensure it will be a boy, you should go with pink ponies and ballerinas," Jake said. "And you should make sure it's very costly and highly time-consuming to change."

"I don't need any insurance," I said. "I told you, I have Agnes."

Besides, nautical can be easily converted to island. Just throw in a dolphin, a few grass skirts at the windows, some silk hibiscus and a lei here and there.

I've never been so excited about decorating a room. The only thing I'm not excited about is trying to find a place for all that junk that's up in the attic. I've decided to bring down a box a day and go through it. I should have it all done in three weeks, when the construction crew is scheduled to start the remodel. With the basement now as a game room, we'll have little storage space, so most of whatever is in those boxes has to go. Most of it should. We've survived this long without even knowing what it is.

Today, I'm on my third box. Katie pulled out a mass of bubble wrap, rolled and taped together to look like a bundle of sausages. "What's in here?" she asked.

"I don't know," I said, "but don't drop it. Whatever it is, it must be very fragile." I cut the tape binding the bubblewurst together and unwrapped one. It was a Lenox Goldfinch.

"Aw, how cute," Katie said, grabbing for another one. "Can I see what's in the rest of them?"

"Yes, carefully," I said. "These are probably collector's items."

"Where did you get them?" she asked, smiling at a meadowlark.

"A friend gave them to me."

"Wow, that was really nice of her," she said. "These are beautiful."

"Yes, they are," I said.

"What's this one?"

"A cerulean warbler," I replied, surprised I remembered.

I wondered if Don Simon still went bird watching. I wondered if he is still married and how many kids he has. Right after I announced my engagement, he announced his, to a woman he had met on an Audubon Society nature outing after I got serious about Jake. Don set his wedding date for three weeks before mine. Every time we saw each other, he threw hints that his fiancé was his second choice -- that he was settling for her because he couldn't have me. I felt sorry for her. I wondered if she

knew. One time, Don called me up to ask me what color Chero-
kee he should buy.

"Did you ask Brenda?" I said.

"No, I wanted to see what *you* think."

"What does it matter what I think?" I said. "You're getting
married in two weeks. Who's the bride anyway?"

"That depends," he said, "on if you'll agree to wear white to
the wedding."

Katie unrolled a kingfisher.

"Can we put this collection up somewhere?" she asked.

"I don't know," I said.

"It's so beautiful," she said. "Can I have it for my room?"

"Is there room in your room for one more thing?" I asked.

"I'll make room, Mom," she said. "These are so nice."

"OK," I said. "They're yours."

"Oh, thank you, thank you, Mom," she said, hugging the
kingfisher. "I promise I'll be very careful not to break them. Really, *really* careful."

"Don't worry. I trust you with them," I said, yawning.
"Let's see what's in this other box."

****

I went for my prenatal check-up this afternoon. When I got
home, I told Jake my C-section was scheduled for March 20.

"The doctor said C-section was the safest way since that's
how Laura was born and I'm not getting any younger," I said.

"You ought to look into having them tie your tubes while
they're in there," Jake said. "That's what Tom and Cecile did
after their third."

"Tie my tubes?"

"Well, there'll be no more scalpels around my family jewels."

The thought of either option hit me as repulsive -- not repulsive as in hideous and disgusting, but repulsive as in repelling
me far away. And I can't even tell you why, except to say that I

felt insulted on behalf of the baby I was carrying. We would allow this child to come into the world for our purposes, but we would accept no more of the likes of him, because any more would not be useful to our plans. That is exploitation, not love. Since I couldn't articulate any of this with any sense of logic sufficient for a conversation with Jake, I said nothing. I hoped something would happen between now and March 20 to avert us from the path we had once taken and lived to regret.

16

DEATH AND LIFE CONVERGING

We will be flying back to Minneapolis on Sunday for John Joseph Lovely's funeral.

"Frannie sends her condolences," I told Jake, swiping Mascara over my lashes. "She is planning to be at the funeral."

"Oh, that's nice," Jake said, scraping the shaving cream from his chin with a Bic. "You should try to get away and spend some time with her while we're there."

"No, that's OK," I said. I threw my mascara back in the drawer and ambled over to Jake. I rubbed his shoulders as I talked to him in the mirror. "We'll be busy with family. I'll plan a trip to catch up with friends some other time."

"There really isn't that much family," Jake said. "I'm sure you'll be able to cut loose for an evening. Maybe we'll make it a foursome with her and Brad."

"I thought you didn't like Brad."

"He's an OK guy," Jake said, rinsing off the razor. "Just kind of intense."

I can see why Jake Lovely would think that about Brad Jones. Brad, a bankruptcy attorney, is driven and meticulous. The Jones home never had so much as a fingerprint on the walls, and Brad was a master gardener in his spare time. So while Jake preferred to talk about who scored the winning run in the World Series game of 2005, Brad wanted to educate the world about the dangers of over-investment, scrubbable flat paint that really isn't scrubbable at all, and root rot.

Jake was still holding the razor under the water. He was staring into the sink. I stared with him, watching the bubbles make their way around the vortex before they were swallowed into the chrome throat of the sink. I noticed in the mirror that Jake's tan face had lost its supple softness. There was a deep, vertical line between his eyebrows. My breasts ached for the soft warmth of his back. I wanted to press my entire body against the whole length of his, but once my belly touched, nothing else could. I hoped the fullness of new life pressing against him might, in some way, mitigate the loss of the old. Death and life, at once, converging. This is how it has gone since the beginning of time and this is the way it will march until the end. I just wish John Joseph could have held his newest grandson.

When Jake got the call that his father had passed away from a heart attack, he clenched his jaw, nodded and said "OK, uh-huh, OK."

I'm not sure if "OK" signaled immediate acceptance on his part or if there was just no other word that came to mind. I put my arms around him from the back and held onto him. I wanted to say and do the right things. It's times like these when you feel like a stranger to your own spouse. You become aware that you indeed are two separate beings, who can't fully suffer for each other, and you become self conscious about that.

I settled on treating Jake like I'd treat any friend who just lost a loved one. I told him about the strange feeling I had when Auntie Bev died -- like I'd been orphaned, even at the age of 42, even though it had been seven years since she was incapacitated -- sequestered in a nursing home -- and more than two decades since she had taken care of me. Still, when she died, I felt alone. I had seen her three weeks before she died. She had acquired a kind of wisdom that I had never before known her to possess.

"Terry, there are things we hold deep inside that we need to tell someone," she said, her boney hand trembling in mine. "Long-kept secrets."

"Yes, Auntie," I said, ready to hear whatever it was she needed to get off her chest.

"Go ahead, Honey," she said. "Tell me anything you like. Tell me so you won't wish that you had after I'm already gone."

"Oh, uh, me?" I said. "I don't know."

"Every child has secrets they've kept from their parents. Or from someone. This would be a good time to tell me. Your secret will surely die with me. Look around. Who am I going to tell?"

I smiled.

"For me," she said, "it was the time I told my parents I was picking up litter for a senior year community service project, when I was actually making out at the home of a boy whose parents were out of town."

"Auntie!" I said.

"It was a long time ago," she said, as if that didn't go without saying, from the lips of a trembling, decrepit old woman.

"So," she said. "What do you got?"

"OK," I said. "You know how Lily always used to dial 911?"

"Oh, yes."

"Well, it wasn't always her."

"What? Really?"

"I did it the first time to see what would happen. Then, when I found out how cool it was -- and how cute the firemen were -- I did it again. Every time after that, it was Lily who did it. I guess she thought they were cute too."

"Oh, Terry," Auntie said. "Do you know how much grief that whole 911 thing caused me? And to think Lily got the idea from you."

"I know, Auntie," I said. "I'm sorry."

"I know you can't tell because my face doesn't work, Terry Honey, but I'm smiling right now."

I hugged her and the tremors from her Parkinson's rattled our embrace.

"I thought those firemen were pretty cute myself," she said.

I grabbed her hand and looked into her eyes. "I'm going to miss you, Auntie," I said. "But we'll see each other again."

"I don't know, Doll," she said. "I am pretty sick."

"I know," I said. "I mean we'll see each other up there." I raised my eyebrows to the ceiling.

"No, that's the labor and delivery floor," she said. "I'm too old and too darned tired to push out a baby."

"Auntie! You know what I mean."

"Yes, Love," she said, putting her hand on my cheek. "I'll see you up there." She tipped her chin up slightly as she said it. Then she laid her hand on mine and closed her eyes.

"Auntie?"

"Yes, Love." She didn't open her eyes.

"Will you say hello to Mom for me?"

"You bet." She squeezed my hand and began to snore.

****

I don't relish the thought of traveling right now. I haven't been feeling my best, but funerals never come at a convenient time. I do look forward to paying tribute to the wonderful father of the wonderful man I married.

John Joseph Lovely enlisted in the U.S. Air Force when he was 18 and fought in two wars by the time he was 30. Two years after returning from Iraq, he married Michelle Bailey, a fourth grade school teacher. The couple had two sons, who both married and fathered four children each. John Lovely took care of his ailing wife until she died of cervical cancer at the age of 57. John got remarried a year later to a woman he met through a support group for people who have lost loved ones to cancer. After three years, she separated from him, saying that she was unable to love another man the way she loved her late husband. Neither one of them ever filed for divorce and are still legally married to this day, although as far as anyone can tell, there's been no contact between the two of them in more than four years. It will be interesting to see if she comes to the funeral.

We haven't been back to Minneapolis since we moved to Seattle. We decided to stay a couple of extra days so we could see old friends. Part of me can't wait to see Frannie. The other part is nervous. Frannie and I met more than two decades ago at a fraternity party. We found instant camaraderie in our mutual rolling of eyes at the drug-induced mating rituals of undergrads. Our dates were best friends with each other and proceeded to paw indiscriminately at practically every girl with breast implants, leaving the two of us B-cups to reflect on what dogs we were dating. Somehow the hash brownie plate and the ecstasy chaser had passed us by, and we were the only two in the room who failed to see the wisdom in having an experience you will never remember and catching a disease you will never get rid of. Frannie and I ended up leaving and driving to a Denny's for a 2 a.m. breakfast.

I don't want to give the impression that we were exactly level headed back then. If we were, we wouldn't have been at that ridiculous party in the first place, in the company of the two losers we were dating.

There are a few universal truths about female relationships. One is that every woman has a crazy friend from her past. This would be the one she met when she had few responsibilities and no commitments. When she had hours to donate on the phone, offering encouragement on meeting the right man or getting published or landing a part in the community play. Back in the days when she had whole evenings to spend, sitting on the floor at the coffee table, back propped against the sofa, shoes kicked off, eating Chinese food right out of the box, listening to stories of childhood dysfunction and adolescent adventures. It was when she had time to sop up a torrent of tears over the latest lost love and then drive through the dark of night to a 24-hour coffee shop to procure a large wedge of seven-layer chocolate cake, which was then to be methodically disfigured by the forks of two women hoping to dig decadent comfort from it while the rest of the world sleeps. For me, this friend was Frannie.

If this friend happens to find someone crazy enough to marry her, and she has children and moves into a suburban home, she loses her status as a crazy friend and joins the ranks of ordinary people whom you have dinner with once every two months at a trendy bohemian restaurant that serves an eclectic, cross-culinary mix of healthy foods. This is termed "Moms' Night Out," which means, in all likelihood, your children will be watching a video and eating pizza rolls at home with their fathers while you and your friend talk about the frequency of bowel movements in young children and the limited-time two-for-one deal at the museum for youth. If, on the other hand, your friend does not marry, she remains crazy, and your husband feels he must protect you from her because she has earned a notorious reputation for overstepping boundaries.

Another universal truth about female friendship is that -- irrespective of race, religion, age, socioeconomic background or country of origin -- every woman wants an Ethel. An Ethel is someone who will not only show up at your door unannounced, she will enter without knocking. She will proceed to your coffee pot, reach into your dishwasher for a mug and seat herself at your kitchen table. She does all of this without a formal greeting because she left the day before without a formal parting. This is because your friendship floats along on one long, streaming, winding, meandering conversation with no end and a beginning that cannot be recalled. Your Ethel tells you when you've got a harebrained idea and after you disregard her warnings, helps you clean up the mess. Your Ethel makes you laugh when you're upset for ridiculous reasons and encourages you to cry when you're sad because you ought to be.

Finding an Ethel is not easy, partly because most women don't know how to be an Ethel, partly because of geographical constraints (your would-be Ethel may live too far to make your coffee pot easily accessible), and partly because -- and this is a big one -- your Ethel must be married to your husband's Fred. You can imagine how remote these odds are.

I, like most American women, do not have an Ethel. I've searched all my adult life for one. Whenever I meet a new friend, I wonder, could this one be it? She never is. Frannie is my best friend. But she is not an Ethel. First off, she is not married to a Fred. Second, I don't trust her implicitly. She has too often given me the wrong advice, especially about men. An Ethel is wiser than you are, and she talks you out of things, not into them. Still, Frannie is my best friend because no matter how I feel, she gets it. Or at least up until now.

For the first time since I met Frannie, I am quite certain that there is finally something about me she won't get. She won't get my big belly. She's seen my belly big three times, but that was before she convinced me to convince Jake to take steps to assure that such a thing never happens again. The pill is bad for your body, she said, but a quick snip will do the trick. Brad had gotten it done after their two children and there was nothing to it, she had said. Jake was reluctant at first.

"It seems so final," he said.

"Well, it is final," I said. "That's the point."

"And that's what you want?"

"Don't you think two kids is enough?" I said.

"I guess so," he said. "It's just that this is such a forever decision."

I wondered if he was considering remarrying someday.

"Do you want another baby?" I asked.

"No," he said.

"Well, then."

"OK," he said. "You win."

He had the vasectomy the following month. The month after that I found out I was pregnant. Katie made it through right under the wire. We did the math and figured out she was conceived two nights before the vasectomy. Jake wasn't upset, but I was. Now I can't imagine our lives without Katie. We would have never heard of the Fujita scale.

****

Yes, black is slimming, but not enough to hide a 21-week pregnancy.

Frannie hugged me, stood back and gawked at my belly.

"We have a lot to catch up on, don't we," she grinned.

"Yeah, I guess we do." I smiled and hugged her tight again.

"How in the world, Terry?"

"I'll explain it all at dinner. It's kind of a long story."

"OK," she said, laying her hand on my tummy. "When's the big day?"

"March 20," I said.

The funeral was typical and beautiful, just like the life of the man it celebrated. Typical with the exception of his estranged wife, sitting in the back of the church, weeping as if she'd lost her one and only soul mate.

The following day we spent with Jake's family. The day after that, we set a time to meet Frannie and Brad for dinner. Frannie called at half past five and told me Brad wouldn't be coming. He had not come to the funeral either. Frannie said he wasn't feeling well. I told Jake that Brad would be a no-show for dinner and he asked if he could stay in and watch the game. He said he was worn out from the wall-to-wall conversation in the past few days and needed some time alone. I understood and was glad because then it would be unabashed girl talk at dinner, which was always much more interesting than girl talk tempered by the presence of a man.

Of course, the first thing Frannie wanted to know was how one of those "little buggers" slipped through and found an egg to fertilize. If she would have felt bold enough, I know she would have asked me if it was someone else's baby.

"Jake had a reversal," I said, talking over my closed menu.

"A reversal?"

"A vasectomy reversal."

"Oh," she said. "Why?"

"So I could get fat like a pregnant lady."

Frannie rolled her eyes. "I mean, why did you want another baby, Terry?"

"Someone was missing," I said. "Like you know how when one of your kids is at a friend's house or something, but you still set a place for them at the table?"

"Yeah."

"It was like that. I was setting places for someone. Not literally, you know." I could tell she didn't get it. "We almost never had Katie, Fran. Remember?"

"Yeah." Frannie smiled.

"She would have been missing." The waiter glanced at me from across the room and I remembered to open my menu. "So this extra dinner plate I always want to set. It must mean something, don't you think?"

"It means you are a woman close to menopause, who sees her fertility winding down and wants to squeeze in one more baby to keep her among the ranks of young mothers. I can understand that, Terry. Believe me. I've had those kind of days. But I just call my plastic surgeon."

"So your theory is that we spent $10,000 on a vasectomy reversal to indulge my mid-life crisis?"

"Hey, that's cheap. Do you know how much a fanny lift costs?"

"Haven't a clue," I said.

We tried to catch up in a lot of different ways, but it was hard, with so much ground to cover. Toward the end of the evening, we got around to talking about our marriages. I told Frannie that Jake is the same old Jake. Still no chance of him changing a light bulb. Frannie told me she is having an affair and that her marriage to Brad is -- for all intents and purposes -- over. Although I wouldn't have been four years ago, I was shocked tonight. I was all set up in my mind to silently judge her, until I remembered my glass house. I had almost forgotten that I had once fantasized about leaving Jake. I had a sudden loss of appetite and put down my fork. The thought of what I could have destroyed -- and what Frannie already did -- made my head swim. And even though it's been a decade since I last felt them, I could not mistake the sudden familiar pains of labor.

17

THE GREAT MYSTERY

"This can't be happening," I panted. "I'm only 21 weeks. Please, God, don't let this be happening. Please, Jesus. Mother Mary, please. Agnes, please help him."

It was Frannie who was sitting next to me, holding my hand. But it was Nina's face I saw.

"Hail Mary, full of grace, the Lord is with thee. Blessed art thou among women, and blessed is the fruit of thy womb Jesus. Holy Mary, mother of God, pray for us sinners, now and at the hour of our death." I prayed alone.

Frannie had driven me to the E.R., and we were waiting for the verdict from the doctor. We had been unable to reach Jake, who I imagined must have taken everyone down to the hotel lounge to grab a bite, leaving his cell phone on the nightstand.

"It's going to be OK, Terry," Frannie reassured me.

I began to cry, and felt hysteria overtake me. "I've never been early before, Frannie. Why would this be happening?"

"Just try to relax, Terry," she said, rubbing my forehead. "The baby's going to be fine."

I wanted to believe her, and I probably would have yesterday. But how do you trust anything from the mouth of a woman who cheats on her husband?

When Frannie was finally able to notify Jake, she relinquished her post at my bedside to him.

By then, the nifedipine had kicked in and arrested the labor. The doctor sent me and Jake back to the hotel the next morning, with the prediction that when we returned home, my ob/gyn would put me on bed rest. As for the airplane trip, he said, a one-hour flight on the Concorde should not be harmful, as long as the labor pains haven't returned by boarding time. The last thing I wanted was to deliver a pre-term baby 60,000 feet in the air. And the second to the last thing I wanted was to be stuck in Minneapolis for the remainder of my pregnancy and/or through-out the baby's NICU stay. I figured my chances of keeping the baby in were not going to get any better from here on out, so Jake stuffed belongings into suitcases, amidst the children's whines and groans that no one would be able to see old friends. When Jake looked into my eyes and told me our baby was going to stay put for another 19 weeks, I believed him.

While we waited at the terminal, we watched a little girl splayed out in the middle of the floor, as if it was her own living room, surrounded by crayons, coloring a Scooby-Doo picture. I couldn't help but think of Tasha. How I missed that kid. Her voice replayed itself in my head and I had to laugh, while tears stung my eyes.

"The man talked to the banana and fell in the coffee," she'd say. "That's the joke I made up. That's a funny one."

As soon as I stepped foot in our house, pre-term labor re-sumed. We rushed off to my doctor, who gave me another shot and put me on bed rest. The next day, I called Lucy and told her I wouldn't be able to attend classes until after the baby is born. I spent the morning thinking about Nina and all her struggles against the system and wondered if my baby was fated for the same fight. The phone rang. It was Nina. Father Fitz had told her to come pray with me. An hour later, she was in my family room with me -- with her two beautiful girls -- praying the rosary. Then she spoke to Sophia. She asked her to look out for John Jacob.

"I'm so sorry you lost her," I said, after we had prayed. I could hardly speak the words through the tears that suddenly overtook me.

"Sophia is a Greek word for 'wisdom,'" she told me. "We have to trust in a wisdom far greater than ours."

"I know," I said. "But how do you go on each day?"

"Knowing her life made a difference," she said.

I wanted to ask how it made a difference, but it seemed like a ridiculous question to ask a mother. Of course, every child changes you. Makes you better or stronger or more patient or more humble. Makes your heart soar and ache to a height and depth you never knew existed. So I wasn't going to ask her that ridiculous question. But I do wonder what difference a two-pound, one-month life made in this world.

Later, Lily served me my dinner -- a tuna noodle casserole Nina had left for the kids to pop in the oven. Alongside it on the tray was a play-dough sculpture of a baby lying on a mound of straw. I burst into tears at the thought of Lily's stubby fingers rolling each piece of tiny yellow dough into strands. The baby was light pink, crude and primitive, with a head far too large for its body, making it look like a 16-week fetus. My heart ached for it. As good as I'm certain Nina's cooking is, I couldn't bring myself to eat. I picked up my book and read John Paul II's words.

According to the Bible, the conception and birth of a new human being are accompanied by the following words of the woman: "I have brought a man into being with the help of the Lord." (Gen. 4:1). This exclamation of Eve, the mother of all the living, is repeated every time a new human being comes into the world. It expresses the woman's joy and awareness that she is sharing in the great mystery of eternal generation. The spouses share in the creative power of God!

****

Beth drove me to my 28-week doctor's visit. Jake was meeting with a client across town. My obstetrician told me everything was looking good and that I need to lighten up. He said I'm going to do more harm than good with my worrying. I told him I was scared to death that the medical staff would not provide my baby treatment if he is born too early or too sick.

"Oh, you don't have to worry about that," he said. "Anyone born after 24 weeks is automatically assumed viable. Ever since Sophia's Law went into effect."

"Sophia's Law?"

"Yes. A woman recently sued the system when her preemie was denied care. She had had two other children that had survived with medical intervention, but her third was denied care and died. The court ruled in her favor. Now the state requires doctors to try to save any preemie born later than 24 weeks. So you're good."

The doctor typed notes into his hand-held as he spoke. "Now, let's see, Terry. Have we talked about contraceptive options? Tubal ligation?"

"No," I said, "I don't think so." I was still processing the news about Sophia as the doctor rattled on.

"It's something you may want to consider. It would be a fast procedure that wouldn't add any recovery time to your C-section. Many women your age -- and with the number of children you have -- find it a good option for them. It is, however, a permanent contraceptive. You need to be certain that you will not want any more children."

"Well, I don't have a very good track record on being certain of such things."

"Well, we've got time. Just let me know after talking it over with your husband. I'll just make a note to follow up at our next visit," he said, clicking at his computer. "Sound good?"

I hope Jake won't bring it up again. If he does, I don't know if I will be able to say no to him, after all the yeses he's given me. But something deep within me shudders at the thought of destroying our fertility -- after all we've gone through to restore it. I just pray Jake somehow comes to the same conclusion.

****

This afternoon, I scheduled Lily's outpatient surgery for seven weeks after my C-section. Lily wanted to call Pablo, so she could tell him she was having her hernia repaired. After a half hour of catching him up on all the news, including a detailed list of all the new dishes she has learned to prepare since I've been on bed rest, Lily passed the phone to me.

"Terry, how are you Mija?"

"Fine, Pablo," I said. "How are you? It's so good to hear your voice."

"Yours too, Mija. How is that little baby of yours? He's giving you trouble already, eh?"

"Boys will be boys, I guess."

"I've been thinking about you every day, filling the head of your angel de la guardia with ideas on how to make you at peace."

"Thank you, Pablo," I said. "It's working. I am at peace."

"Listen, Lily tells me she's having an operation. Would you mind if I come and lend a hand?"

"Not at all," I said. "That would be great."

"OK, I'll plan on it," he said. "I'll book a hotel room and stay for a few days."

"Don't you dare," I said. "I will not have any member of our family staying in a hotel when we have a perfectly good guest room." We actually don't have a guest room, but Katie's serves as a makeshift. She can room with Laura.

"You'll have your hands full already, Terry, I don't want--"

"Nonsense," I said. "You will stay here. We'll need another pair of hands to hold the baby."

"OK, Mija, OK. Thank you. Thank you for letting me be there for Lily. I've never been able to take care of her. I owe her at least this much. Myself too."

"I'm sure she'll find it very comforting to have you here," I said.

After we hung up, I picked up my John Paul II book to read myself sleepy.

"Let each one of you love his wife as himself. And let the wife see that she respects her husband. Respect, because she loves and knows she is loved in return. It is because of this love that husband and wife become a mutual gift. Love contains the acknowledgment of the personal dignity of the other, and of his or her absolute uniqueness. Indeed, each of the spouses, as a human being, has been willed by God from among all the creatures of the earth for his or her own sake. Each of them, however, by a conscious and responsible act, makes a free gift of self to the other and to the children received from the Lord."

Suddenly I felt a wave of panic rush over me. All these years, I had gotten it wrong -- or at least only half right. In my egocentric view, I had always thought my husband and my children were given to me. I had never considered that, through a conscious act of my own, I might be a gift to them.

****

The ultrasound tech told us our son was sucking his right thumb. Jake said that was a sign of exceptional coordination -- that all the great athletes were known to have been in-utero thumb suckers.

"Actually," the tech said, playing along, "Thumb sucking is quite common. Sucking the toes, however, has been linked with both mental and physical prowess. Let's hope we see some toe-sucking next time."

The OB was just impressed that the baby was staying put. He had counted on the "little guy" being in the NICU by now, he said. He reviewed his notes and noticed that the question of tubal ligation was still unanswered.

"Oh, yeah, we'll take it, doc," Jake told him. "As a matter of fact, we'll take two. We've got a houseful, right Babe?" He looked at me and rubbed my back softly with the tips of his fingers.

"I think that's a wise choice," the doctor said, making notes. "You don't want to have to go in later and make another incision and face more recovery time."

And so, with my silent consent, the fate of future generations was sealed unto eternity.

****

Finally, at 36 weeks, I am allowed off bed rest. I decided to try to make one last meeting at Queen of Peace before the C-section lays me up.

"St. Paul's letter to the Ephesians refers to family life as "a great mystery because it expresses the spousal love of Christ, the Bridegroom, for his Church, the bride," Lucy said, switching her nursing baby onto her other breast. She picked up the book on John Paul II's Letter to Families and read:

"Modern rationalism does not tolerate mystery. It does not accept the great mystery proclaimed in the Letter to the Ephesians, but radically opposes it. It may well acknowledge, in the context of a vague deism, the possibility and even the need for a supreme divine being, but it firmly rejects the idea of a God who became man in order to save man. For rationalism, it is unthinkable that God should be Redeemer, much less that he should be the Bridegroom, the primordial and unique source of the human love between spouses. Rationalism provides a radically different way of looking at creation and the meaning of human existence. But once man begins to lose sight of a God who loves him ... and once the family no longer has the possibility of sharing in the great mystery, what is left except the mere temporal dimension of life? Earthly life becomes nothing more than the scenario of a battle for existence, of a desperate search for gain, and financial gain before all else."

And the changing of light bulbs.

WHEREVER LILY GOES

****

Nine days before my scheduled C-section, I went into labor. I called Jake at a Sonics game. He bolted through the door less than 45 minutes later, panting and puffing, like he was the one about to give birth. Trailing him was a stream of frantic girls. I chuckled as I imagined them taking three bleachers at a time, bounding ground-ward with their long muscular Lovely legs, oblivious to the dirty looks from annoyed fans, startled by the harsh vibrations stunning their backsides. As Jake helped me into the car, I reminded him we had to make a stop at the grocery store to get Lily.

"Babe," he said. "Do you think that's a good idea? What if we don't make it?"

"I don't think we have any other choice, Honey," I said. "Lily has to be there for this."

Beth ran in to get Lily while we waited at the curb. Seeing Lily shoot out of those automatic doors made me wonder why she never entered the running events of Special Olympics.

Jake drove like a New York City cab driver. And still, with all the haste this family could muster, that baby wanted to be born right there in the front seat of our SUV, bulleting along Interstate 5 at speeds approaching 80 mph. By the time we got to the hospital, his head was crowning and they decided to let me go ahead and try to push him out instead of prepping me for a C-section. No time for an epidural, but the nurse told me to think of something that makes me happy, so I thought of Tasha and one of her ridiculous jokes:

"The nose and the mouth had a party and danced with the alligator. And the alligator told them that "A" starts with apple and they all ate pie. How do you like that one?"

The strange thing is, the pains of childbirth weren't nearly as bad as I had remembered them. After forty-five minutes of pushing, the OB stepped aside, and Jake caught the latest Lovely, his first son, while Lily looked on over his right shoulder, her

178

hands clasped tight together, springing on her toes in anticipation of holding the smallest human being she'd ever seen.

"Look at this kid," Jake said, tilting our crying baby in my direction. "He looks like a linebacker. Good thing he didn't stay in another three weeks."

"You're telling me," I said. John Jacob Lovely's headlong rush through the birth canal changed the game plan and saved my tubes.

"Yup," the doctor said, wiping his brow with the back of his glove, "We can make all the plans we want, but in the final analysis, the moment at which each person enters and leaves this world is tied into the great mystery of life."

He glanced at the nurse who was typing into a hand-held. "Three sixteen p.m.," he said.

Three sixteen. John 3:16. It is the only Bible verse I know by memory -- the one printed on the bottom of Forever XXI shopping bags and on bumper stickers and little rubber bracelets. "For God so loved the world that He gave His one and only Son..."

"Aw, just look at him, Babe." Jake shook his head and blinked back tears.

"Can my girls come in now?" I asked the nurse.

"Of course," she said. "I'll get them."

Laura and Katie broke into high-pitched squeals at the sight of their brother.

"How adorable.

"How tiny."

"I want to hold him."

"Look at all his hair."

"He looks like a Chia Pet."

Beth stood in silence, wiping her face, trying to keep up with the massive amounts of mascara streaming down her cheeks. It wasn't working. She hadn't let anyone see her cry since that night at the cricket-infested motel. Her eyes met mine and I burst into tears.

"He look like me," said Lily.

The doctor clamped the umbilical cord and handed the scissors to Jake. Lily rested her hand on top of Jake's, smiling the widest I've ever seen. Laura readied a camera, pointing the lens at the fleshy, red baby Jake had placed on my belly. The snip of the scissors was about to ring in something entirely new. And every one of us in that room -- intoxicated with the sweet, earthy smell of childbirth -- knew it.

About the Author

Sherry Boas began her writing career in a hammock in a backyard woods in rural Massachusetts when she was eight years old, writing a "novel" about the crime-fighting abilities of her Cocker Spaniel. Fourteen years later, she would draw her first writer's paycheck for a very different kind of story when she landed a job at a newspaper in Arizona. She spent the next decade as a journalist, winning news awards, but her heart still belonged to fiction. So, after twelve years at home with her four adopted and highly inspiring children, the words to the Lily trilogy found themselves onto these pages. *Wherever Lily Goes* is the second in the trilogy. *Until Lily* and *Life Entwined with Lily's* are also available from Caritas Press. Visit www.lilytrilogy.com.